MW00356496

Music Lessons

Frances Walker

Copyright © 2013 Frances Walker
All rights reserved.

ISBN: 0615954324
ISBN 13: 9780615954325
Library of Congress Control Number: 2014900989
Frances Walker, Gardenale, AL

With love to Looie.....who made it possible.

Prologue

Even after thirty years, it still stuck in her craw.

Just how Bertie El had ended up in this insignificant, blue-collar, pitiful little town in the foothills of East Tennessee had to be a joke.

And how she, Roberta Ellen Dabney-- once a belle from Richmond, Virginia-- could be the dowdy, thick-waisted, middle-aged, ol' Mrs. Hewitt of Riverview Heights was just a bad dream, a near nightmare that she awoke to every blessed day now. No matter how she tried, no matter how often she stood in her lovely, whitewashed sun-room, sipping tea from her grandmother's Limoges cups, wearing Ferragamo pumps, and admiring her rose garden, Bertie El still came back to it. She was stunned—at herself and her life. The shock of it never seemed to wear- off.

Never mind that she lived on a picture-book knoll above the river in one of the finest houses in East Tennessee, built in 1919 of native stone and heart pine. And never mind that, compared to most of the people residing within a hundred miles, Bertie El Hewitt had plenty of money and no big problems that anyone knew of. She had a housemaid, a gardener, a big new '61 Buick, and a glossy grand piano that could be seen through the huge front windows of the fine house on Riverview Road.

Ask anyone in Grantville—they could tell you—ol' Mrs. Hewitt was a widow now, she had no children, she denied having birthdays, and she attended All Saints Episcopal Church.

"And for twenty years now I've been trying to teach music to the hopeless urchins of this pathetic, little town," Bertie El had been known to comment after an extra glass of sherry.

I was one of those urchins, and I dreamed of that big, glossy piano.

1

The Hewitt house on Riverview had always been a palace to me. Along with dozens of other kids from the mill village down in the valley, on Halloween I always made a point of climbing the hill to trick-or-treat at the "big houses," as we called them. I would stand among the crowd on the wide front porch, each of us wearing some ridiculous homemade costume, and hold out my brown paper grocery bag as Evelyn, the colored maid, dropped handfuls of candy toward us.

I always lingered there, taking time to look long and hard beyond the huge front door or through the tall front windows. If I had to, I turned or swayed among my friends in order to see it all—the bright chandeliers, the long, heavy drapes, the patterned rugs, and especially the piano. "They call those kind *grand* pianos," my cousin Maryanne had informed us all one night, and I instantly understood the grand part.

The only pianos I had ever touched or heard in person were old uprights; there were two at Mount Vernon First Baptist Church, and there was one in the auditorium of Crocker Elementary School. As far as I knew, no one else in Grantville, Tennessee, had any other kind—no one, that is, but Mrs. Hewitt.

At Crocker Elementary School, beginning in third grade, we had music twice a week for thirty minutes in the auditorium with Miss Clark, who traveled around the county. Nothing thrilled me more than watching her play that piano. I always sat where I could watch Miss Clark's hands, and sometimes at the end of class, I would stay behind, standing beside her as she played while the class filed out. She smiled at my interest.

I watched—no, I stared—mesmerized, all through third and fourth grade. Sometimes after school I would sneak into the auditorium to spend a few minutes at the keyboard, until Mrs. Wright from the office would come tell me to get on home.

I loved the piano—any piano. I loved the pattern of the smooth white keys topped by the long, skinny black ones; I loved the tingle and shimmer of the sounds that stretched well past the reach of my right hand, and I loved the deep, dark rumble that came from my left.

Alone in the auditorium one afternoon, I once dragged a stool to the back of the old worn-out upright and stood on it, struggling to lift the heavy lid of the instrument. I wanted to see where those sounds came from; I wanted to see what made them. The wires and hammers deep inside formed an amazing design to me, and I wanted so much to somehow play a note and be able to watch what happened inside at the same time.

But the sudden sound of grown-up footsteps coming toward the door put an end to my exploration. I closed the lid, jumped down from the stool, and hurried on my way.

Every chance I got, both at school and at church, I sat at the piano and picked and punched at the keys. If someone was playing a piano, I was right there, absorbed in watching their fingers. I watched closely, and I began to memorize some of the endless combinations that made the white keys and the black keys fit together in an order that made the sounds blend and become music.

The more I watched, the more sense it all made. I saw that there were basic patterns and groups of notes that I could use to make a game, and the game, once unraveled a bit, could be applied to make a song.

By my tenth birthday, I could play lots of the songs I had watched other people play.

The more I played my piano game, the more closely I could listen and pick out the sounds of each pattern. The brightness or sadness of certain notes became keenly familiar to me. My piano game got easier, but had I been asked, or told, to explain the game, I couldn't have. The game felt a little twisted and fuzzy in my head, and I knew that no one would ever understand or believe it if I did try to talk about it.

But what they did believe was that I, Grace Stevens, could play the piano and that I "had never had the first lesson."

"She plays by ear," my grandmother told her neighbors.

"Never had a lesson...and can't read a note of music," my Sunday School teacher told the preacher's wife after I played "Onward Christian Soldiers" every morning of Vacation Bible School assembly. And at the eighth-grade graduation, I, a lowly fifth grader, was called on to play "My Country 'Tis of Thee" when the oldest Hodges girl got sick with a stomach virus.

"I'm tellin' you the truth, Hoyt," Aunt Doris told my daddy one night. "I took Grace into the parlor of the YWCA with me today, and if that young 'un' didn't sit down at the spinet and play 'Rock of Ages,' I'm not standin' here." Aunt Doris went on to tell Daddy that I was a natural talent and that if he had any sense, he wouldn't buy another shotgun or fishing rod or bottle of whiskey until there was a piano in our house.

I knew there was a better chance that I'd find a circus train in our house before I'd ever find a piano, but now I knew about that "spinet" word. That fancy white piano, with the matching velvet bench, that I had played while I waited for Aunt Doris was a spinet.

So there were uprights, spinets, and grands—and I became fairly confident that my game would work on all of them.

2

~

All my life I had known that my mother did not like me, but I clung, like a little bull dog, to the idea that surely she loved me. At least in front of other people she appeared to, anyway. I knew my mother wanted something, and I knew it had something to do with me and my little brother, Wesley. I just couldn't figure out whether she wanted something from us, or for us.

It didn't take long for Momma to hear all about me playing the piano. She cornered me in the kitchen one morning and wanted to know who had taught me to play.

"Nobody," I said. "I just watched... and made-up a game."

She looked at me hard, which was not unusual at all, but didn't say a word. I finished my chocolate milk and waited to see if she'd say anything....anything at all, but she didn't.

Late that night, she and Daddy had another war. This time they had a knock-down-drag-out, call-the-law, hide-the-guns, screamin' and shoutin' match, because Momma announced that she was going to buy me a piano with the money he planned to spend on a new rifle.

I lay in my bed, dead still, listening. Wesley, the soundest-sleeping child ever born, according to my grandmother, lay curled on his little daybed in the corner of our room, stirring only once during the whole ruckus.

I was terrified at the yelling and cursing that filled our tiny two-bedroom mill house, but I was thrilled at the possibility, the mere chance, that I might actually come home from school one day and find a piano in our little living room.

But a month later, Daddy came home with a new rifle. For several days not a word passed between my parents. The tension in our house was scary, and for several nights I lay awake a long time, listening for the sounds of another battle, but none came.

Soon I put the thought of having a piano out of my head. At school and at church, I still took every opportunity to watch and listen and play anytime I could, but I knew better than to say one word to anyone about ever having a piano.

Toward the end of school that May, the principal allowed Miss Clark to send a note home, recommending to my parents that I be given music lessons. Momma read the note and quietly wadded it up before dropping it into the kitchen garbage under the sink. Then she picked up her next Lucky Strike.

"You go back and tell that Miss Clark"—Momma paused as she lit up—"that it don't make sense for a kid who don't have a piano to take music lessons." She turned away, looking for her ashtray, and I knew that was the end of that.

It had been Richard Hewitt's idea for Bertie El to teach piano.

After sixteen years of marriage and no children, he knew his wife needed something—something other than playing bridge and tennis, running the church altar guild, and sipping sherry with the wives of the other mill executives.

Bertie El was an accomplished pianist and equestrian. At age five she had begun piano and riding lessons the same week. By her seventeenth birthday, she was a skilled, blue-ribbon horsewoman and was accepted to the prestigious Virginia Academy of Music, where she studied music theory and the classics.

Her favorite photograph of herself showed her on stage at the National Theatre in Washington, DC. These days the picture—still hanging on the wall of Richard's den—was something Bertie El did not let herself look at very often. In it, she is wearing a simple white evening gown; her hand is resting on the concert grand piano at which she had just performed Brahms's Intermezzo Op. 118. She is twenty years old. No, she is a *glorious* twenty years old, and the footlights glow at her feet as she glances up into the balcony of the crowded concert hall, filled with booming applause, to which she had just bowed gracefully when the camera flashed. It was taken in June 1925.

Two years later the camera flashed again, capturing a bride and groom, Mr. and Mrs. Richard Hewitt, floating down the stairs of Saint Andrews Chapel, followed by eight groomsmen and eight bridesmaids wearing blue silk organza. The Dabney girl's June wedding and reception were front-page news for the *Richmond Courier*.

Her first years of married life with Richard were full of travel and parties and hunts and tennis. They moved into a newly constructed apartment building, located on the back side of the Richmond Country Club, where other young couples were living. They began working on the plans for the house they would build.

Nothing changed immediately for Bertie El in the months after October 1929, but by the summer of 1931, Hewitt Coal and Gas was almost out of business. The company's founder, Richard's grandfather, died suddenly at age seventy-nine; five weeks later, Bertie El's fifty-three-year-old father-in-law, Richard Hewitt Sr., facing the stress of financial ruin, collapsed with a massive stroke. He lived for one month after, during which the last of the Hewitt's family fortune was either forfeited or lost completely.

Bertie El and Richard did not build their new house.

For three years young Richard and Bertie El lived with Mother Hewitt, until Richard was at last employed by a company in Grantville, Tennessee. It was a new factory that would specialize in the production of sheet metal. Sheet metal? thought Bertie El. Of all things, Richard Hewitt, one of the Richmond Hewitts-- if you could believe it--was going into the manufacture of *sheet metal*—and he was taking his young, stunned wife to live someplace she had never heard of in Tennessee.

The first years in Grantville were often touch and go, but by 1939 Crocker-Hewitt Manufacturing was running three full shifts and sales were constantly increasing as war in Europe was nearing. Richard and the company's founder, Burton Crocker, became full partners.

Just a few weeks before Pearl Harbor, Richard and Bertie El moved into the grand, old stone house that had once belonged to Judge Griffis. Richard built a tennis court behind the old barn. He bought two horses and boarded them nearby, for Bertie El to ride, and he became a founding member of the new Winnatoska Golf and Country Club.

Bertie El did not complain. There was, after all, a world war going on, and she was raised better than to whine and grumble about such relatively insignificant things as having no good dress shops and no local arts council when almost every day another gold-star banner appeared in another home around East Tennessee.

Like everybody, Bertie El hoped and prayed for the war to end, but she knew in her bones that even when it did, things would never, ever, be the same. The hard truth was that all the hoping and praying she could ever do was *not* going to get her out of Grantville, Tennessee.

One winter evening in 1943, Bertie El finished playing a Beethoven sonata and turned to see Richard standing in the doorway. She smiled at him, pleased that he had been listening.

He walked toward her and stopped in the middle of the foyer's blue oriental rug. With a slight smile, he pushed his hands deep into his trouser pockets and spoke. "Sweetie...it's time for you to share some of that with someone besides me...and the help. I want you to do something with that magnificent talent of yours. Why not start teaching piano?"

Yes, it had all been Richard's idea.

But the problem was that so many of the town's children came from down in the valley. They were the kids of the mill workers, from families who lived paycheck to paycheck, and the very thought of those ragamuffins—those ill-bred imps, with their poor grammar, grimy, little fingers, and hand-me-down shoes—sitting at Bertie El's superb Feurich grand piano was simply out of the question.

"Honestly, Richard," Bertie El protested, "you surely don't expect me to try to give lessons to these wretched little trolls right here in our front parlor."

It did not take much time to convert the old sleeping porch into a nice little teaching studio.

Even Bertie El had to admit that her studio was a charming little nook. The workmen came and painted the whole room a soft, warm white. Bertie El brought two old oriental carpets down from the attic to cover the old plank flooring then added some plants and an old print she found in a junk store. Two used console pianos were purchased in Knoxville, cleaned and tuned to near perfection, and placed against the large inside wall. Bookshelves for music books and sheet-music collections lined one wall, and there were several old floor lamps that were put to use.

All in all, it was a pleasant alcove. Richard arranged for the landscape man to put down a little stone path around the side of the house so that the students did not tramp through the house, and the large, old magnolia provided ample shade over the studio on hot afternoons. Bertie El was pleased but had her doubts about whether it would work out as Richard hoped.

After Bertie El announced to her Sunday school class that she was going to start teaching piano, the word spread quickly. Her first three students began in the fall; there was the ten-year-old Cunningham boy and the Hanson twins, Judy and Joanie, age nine. Bertie El decided to limit her studio hours to the afternoons, four days a week. After all, she still wanted time to play bridge, ride, do Garden Club, and continue her church work.

By Christmas of that year, every single forty-five-minute afternoon slot was taken, and there was a waiting list of parents leaving their phone numbers in hopes of getting their children signed-up with Mrs. Hewitt. Bertie El was surprised and encouraged, and, of course, Richard was thrilled.

The years passed as dozens of Grantville's youngsters, many of whom were forced into it, endured weekly lessons with Mrs. Hewitt.

Then, in 1956, Richard Hewitt died suddenly.

3

~

Bertie El---widowed--had every intention, every design under the sun, moon, and stars, to leave Grantville and go back to Virginia; "back home" was what she told everybody. It only made sense, given the fact that she had never liked Tennessee, had never really fit in, and had never really put down any roots. Or had she?

"Well, Bertie, dahlin'...far be it from me to tell you that you can't move anywhere you want..." John David Strickland spoke from behind his desk in the longest, slowest southern drawl most people had ever heard. John David had been one of Richard Hewitt's best friends, and his personal attorney, for over twenty years.

"God knows Richard left you in fine, fine shape, my dear," he continued. "And you may leave Grantville tomorrow and live anywhere you jolly well please, I suppose..."

Bertie El stood looking out the large front windows of John David's law office on the third floor of the old courthouse. She was sick and tired of it all—the meetings, the reports, the recommendations, the ifs, ands, and buts of it all. She missed Richard terribly; she was feeling lost and overwhelmed and wanted to go home to Virginia.

For four solid months, she'd met with lawyers, accountants, investment experts, and about a dozen other people who had been directed, by way of Richard Hewitt's will, to advise and guide Bertie El through the maze of assets and holdings that were now all hers. For the first time in her life, Bertie El's signature held sway over power and profits, the extent of which she had simply not dreamed. Richard had left her a wealthy woman, a woman in charge of a network and a not-insignificant empire of sorts—and that empire was *not* in Virginia.

"But, Bertie, dahlin', why would you do that?"

John David did not miss a beat, although Bertie continued to stand with her back to him.

"I'll grant you that our little town here is not exactly a cosmopolitan mecca, but it's not without its own peculiar kinds of charm...and besides, *this* is where you and Richard shared your life...for many, many years. Like it or not, my dear, Grantville, Tennessee, was *home* to Richard. I realize you might not appreciate my pointin' that out to you, Bertie El, but I have to be honest. Richard built a life here—a damned fine life—made up of considerable financial success and community commitment and many, many, loyal friends. Richard was the proverbial pillar, and he'll be sorely missed...I just don't think it ever dawned on him, sugah, that you'd just walk away from all that."

Bertie El turned around abruptly to glare at John David, who hushed-up immediately. Obviously he had made his point.

"I've had it up to my eyeballs, John David, with it *all*," Bertie El said as she walked over and picked-up her handbag and gloves.

"So I'm leavin'...I'm goin' home to Richmond for a nice, long visit, and I'm not going to worry anymore about what I *should* do or *ought* to do or *must* do or *better* do. I don't *have* to decide anything right now, and I'm not going to."

She jerked-on her gloves.

John David stood up. "Of course you don't, dahlin'...you go right on—"

Bertie El interrupted him.

"So for the next month, if you or anybody else has any urgent—and I *do* mean *urgent*—business that absolutely requires my attention, I'll be at my aunt Claudine's house in Richmond. My housekeeper, Evelyn, has the address and phone number."

John David darted from behind his desk to reach the door and open it for her. Bertie El was moving quicker than he had anticipated.

"By all means, dear Bertie, you go right on and take as long as you need. Visit yo' family; enjoy yo'self; do some shoppin'...whatever suits you, dahlin'. I will *personally* take care of anything at all that comes up," he assured her, leaning down to give her a good-bye peck on the cheek.

Bertie El paused; she really could not bring herself to just storm out. She softened. "Thank you, John David...and give Mary Carson my love."

⁓〇

Bertie El went to Richmond.

Two weeks later, she was back in Grantville, still trying to decide what had changed more: Richmond or herself. Richmond is not the same place I left so many years ago, and God knows I'm not the same woman, she thought. She wouldn't do anything for the time being. She would just give it some time, after all there was no hurry.

Bertie El's closest friends agreed that, although she would never admit it, it was her piano students who really kept her going after that. John David showed- up at her door one day with a little, fluffy white puppy; she named him Schubert. She went back to church, slowly resumed her social calendar, and she continued teaching music... forever complaining that not the first one of her students had ever really shown an ounce of real commitment to the piano.

⁓〇

School ended, and our long summer days began. We played outside. No matter how hot it got, we played outside. No matter how bad the mosquitoes or the chiggers or the flies, we played outside. The mill-village kids went out the door in the morning, and when the streetlights came on in the evening, we each headed home.

Even if it rained, we played outside or gathered on someone's front porch to play Chinese checkers until the rain stopped. For lunch we feasted on peanut-butter and banana sandwiches, lucky cakes, Popsicles, and gallons of cheap, sweet Kool-Aid.

There were kids everywhere—on skates, bicycles, playing ball in the street, playing Tarzan in the camp behind the Musgroves' garage, building forts, climbing, swinging, and jumping on and over anything available. We stayed outside, and we played hard, often pausing only to gulp water from the nearest garden hose.

There was no adult supervision, and there was no adult interference. We settled our own squabbles and disputes; we made our own game rules, and the most trouble anyone got in was for tramping through Mrs. Vines' rose bushes or for throwing a water balloon too close to the newest Steadman baby as he sat in his stroller on the sidewalk, happily sucking on a frozen stick of butter and watching the chaos.

Once or twice a week, a group of us would walk all the way to Schivano's Corner Store, where for fifteen cents we could get a king-size bottle of Coca-Cola and a Goo Goo Cluster candy bar.

Sometimes on the way back, I would insist on walking the long way back to our street in order to pass by old Mrs. Bowers's house. She had a piano in what appeared to be her dining room. Since her front windows and front door were sheltered by a wide, shaded porch, they stayed open all summer long, so her piano could easily be heard from the sidewalk.

If the sound of the piano was clear, we sometimes would sit there on the curb, in the shade of a large chinaberry tree, to finish our Cokes.

I listened closely but could never recognize anything Mrs. Bowers played.

"The Bowers are not Baptists, Grace," Debbie Chandler pointed out one afternoon, licking chocolate off her fingers. "They're Catholics...no tellin' what she's playin'." We all nodded in agreement.

Other than the piano at church, I had no way to even touch a keyboard during the summer months, so sometime after the Fourth of July or so, I secretly began to look forward to school starting again.

One blistering-hot August afternoon, I bounded in the back door and flew into the kitchen, just in time to hear my momma shout into the telephone, "...because my kids ain't never gonna have *nothing* if I don't go to work!" and she slammed the receiver down into the cradle of the wall phone there by the kitchen sink.

She turned then to me, and I could tell she was about to say what she always said during the summer: "What are you doin' in here? Get back outside..."

But before she could speak, I, still huffin' and puffin', managed to deliver the news. "Wesley took a header off the Wiggins's' front porch... he's bleedin' like a stuck hog—"

Momma was out the back door and sprinting down the street, with me right on her heels, before I had time to even wonder who she had slammed the phone down on. A few seconds later, she cut straight through the crowd of kids surrounding Wesley and found Mrs. Wiggins--- Harriett--- bent down on her knees, holding ice in a bloody, wet washcloth on Wesley's mouth and nose.

"He's fine, Arlene...but he's minus two teeth, and this top lip is cut pretty deep." Harriett showed Momma while Wesley whimpered.

Off to the Crocker-Hewitt Medical Dispensary and Clinic we went, just six blocks away. Two hours and five stitches later, we were back home. That night Wesley had ice cream for dinner and put his two baby teeth beneath his pillow.

I lay awake a long time that night, listening to another battle. Daddy somehow thought Momma had something to do with Wesley getting hurt.

"Yeah, Arlene, that's *just* what you need to do...go to work...that way maybe both the young 'uns will end up at the clinic, havin' to be stitched up."

That wasn't fair at all.

Suddenly I heard Momma yank the ironing board out of the hall closet and haul it into the kitchen. That's what she did at night when she was mad—she ironed.

"You know, Hoyt, that's all you ever know to do—blame me. But I'm the one who looks after these kids all day and all night, with no help from you. I do every last thing around here—every *damn* last thing, because if you ain't at the mill, you're either sittin' on a deer stand or holdin' a fishin' pole or bendin' your sorry elbow down at the Cozy Corner. So I'll go to work if I want to...and you can just *kiss my ass*."

And with that, the kitchen door slammed shut.

The next morning Wesley found two shiny dimes under his pillow, and everything-- every dish towel, every sock, every doily—everything that wasn't nailed down in our house, had been ironed.

Three weeks later school started. I went into sixth grade, Wesley started first grade, and Momma went to work at the Buddy Burger out on Highway 119.

Momma made forty-five dollars a week as assistant manager and cook. I looked after Wesley every afternoon, and either Aunt Doris or Grammie checked on us every day until four, when Daddy got home. He made it clear that he did not like Momma not being home, and he often complained about having to watch us or having to drive out to pick her up at six if her friend Polly couldn't bring her home.

Even after working all day, Momma came home and got our dinner, did laundry, mopped and vacuumed, and then packed lunches for the next day.

I looked forward all week to Friday. I really liked Fridays; Momma got paid on Friday afternoons, and Daddy was always "busy" down at the Spotlight or the Cozy Corner, so Aunt Doris would take us to the Buddy Burger, where we would get to eat dinner while we waited for Momma.

On the jukebox at the Buddy Burger was a song Momma really liked; she would always hum it for a while after someone played it. It was also popular on the radio, and she would shush us whenever it came on. "Last Date" by Floyd Cramer was a piano instrumental...that's what the record label said.

After hearing "Last Date" several times, I slowly began to pick it out on the school piano and at church on Wednesday nights before choir practice. It didn't take long for me to have most of it figured out, and then even the eighth graders would stand around when I played.

I loved playing the piano. I loved knowing how to do something that not many kids could do. But I knew that the way I played was not really the right way. I knew I did not use the right fingers, and I knew there was something else missing. I could get the notes, but there was nothing smooth or easy in the music I played. There was a choppy disconnect in the sound that I didn't know how to fix, and I had no idea how to use the piano pedals so that the notes would blend. I guess you could say I *banged* on those keys more than I played them.

Most people were amazed at what I could do, but I really wasn't. My game allowed me to get some reasonable sounds out of the piano, but I wanted to really *know* the piano. I wanted to read music and understand what all the symbols and words meant.

With Momma working, I was given a key to the front door, and all that school year, as soon as Wesley and I got home, I would immediately go back to our little bedroom. I had this silly, irrational hope that one day I would arrive home and somehow a piano would have been magically purchased and miraculously squeezed into the tiny space between the radiator and the closet door in our little room.

But then I would remind myself that pianos cost a lot of money and that Daddy didn't like music, period, and he'd said how he did not want to listen to a kid, "jack hammerin' on a piano every damn day," and that our house hardly had room for us—much less something as big as a piano—and that nobody in this family had ever had a musical bone in their body, so who did I think I was, anyway?

I would get Wesley some Kool-Aid, turn-on *Popeye the Sailor* cartoons for him, and go to the kitchen table to do my arithmetic.

4

According to Aunt Doris, there was a specific moment in time when our ancestral procession took a wrong turn and jumped the track, running us all somehow amok. She always claimed that had her and Daddy's grandmother, Cynthia, had the good sense of a nanny goat, she would never have entangled herself with a Stevens, especially a Stevens whose grandfather had been a full-blooded Cherokee Indian.

"She was a Biddle...her own daddy was elected Tennessee governor; she had a perfect upbringing and was a surefire lady...but threw it all away on a no-good named Billy Lee Stevens," Aunt Doris would often explain, shaking her head as if she would never, ever, understand it, much less get over it.

I never, ever, could understand why she would call her own granddaddy a no-good, but she did, and she must have meant it.

Every time the beautiful, silver five-o'clock teaspoons were brought out of the hall buffet-- which had been in the same spot in Grammie Stevens's house since 1936-- and put to use, whether it be Christmas or Easter or a Sunday-school-class lunch, Aunt Doris had to tell about Cynthia Louise Biddle.

"You know, my grandmother was a Biddle..." she would remind her church friends for the umpteenth time, most of whom knew perfectly well who her, and everybody else's, grandmother was.

So the fine, little silver spoons were set out, right beside the tacky turquoise coffee mugs from Woolworth, and nobody from Mount Vernon First Baptist thought a thing of it.

All my life I had heard the story of how this young, pretty girl named Cynthia had run-off with a young man her family hated and how she had sneaked fourteen silver teaspoons out to take with her, because she and the boy had no money. If that was the case, I always wondered, why were the silver spoons still at Grammie Stevens's house? Why hadn't they been sold or swapped for milk and bread by this Biddle girl? But there they were—big as life—heavy and shiny as always.

What all that had to do with my daddy and momma did not make much sense to me, but Aunt Doris seemed to think that it was a big turning point of some kind for all of us.

Cynthia and Billy Lee had a son they named Billy Jr., and later on he was Wesley's and my Grandpa Billy. I remembered Grandpa Billy pretty well; he was tall and always gave me pocket change. He had worked in the mill. He died when I was in second grade, and there was a small, framed picture of him holding Wesley on his knee at Grammie Stevens's house. Wesley had no memory of Grandpa Billy.

But Aunt Doris and Daddy remembered him all too well; they said he was the biggest hell-raisin' misfit of a daddy anybody ever had. Even Grammie Stevens used to say that her "sweet Billy wasn't fit to live with till he was forty-five years old," to which Aunt Doris would always add, "He was *never* fit to live with, Momma."

Daddy would just mutter under his breath, "Yeah, he was sweet... like horseshit."

"Momma, what's wrong with Daddy's blood?"

I asked this once, when I was about six years old, while I stood, struggling for balance, as she brushed my hair into a ponytail. Momma always yanked and tugged hard at my hair; she said it was a battle, because I had enough hair for three girls. I had spent that afternoon with Aunt Doris, picking new peas and strawberries at the Wilson farm.

"Grace, I'm not gonna tell you again...stand still," Momma muttered, holding two bobby pins and a rubber band in her mouth while she brushed. "...and what in the name of a brass monkey's butt are you talkin' about? There's *nothing* wrong with yo' daddy's blood."

20

Then I explained, as she continued brushing and gathering up my hair, how I heard Aunt Doris talking to one of her friends about "that bad blood in all the Stevens men." Then Momma said, hell yes, Doris was right about that...but it was nothing that concerned me. That must have been the truth, because Daddy's blood didn't seem to give him any trouble that I knew of.

Doris Stevens worked in purchasing at the steel mill. She did not smoke or cuss and would never touch alcohol, not even an occasional glass of homemade wine. She always wore stockings and low-heeled shoes, and most people in Grantville thought of her as a lady. Her sewing and embroidery skills were excellent, and she never married, always living with her widowed mother, and doted on her niece and nephew— me and Wesley.

Aunt Doris was a good friend to my momma, often saying that any woman who could live with Hoyt Stevens deserved to be befriended. Doris was only four years older than Daddy, but to most people she always seemed much older.

So, yes, I guess with her skirts and matching sweaters, her little, used Chevrolet coupe, and, of course, with her Biddle grandmother's silver teaspoons, Aunt Doris was a lady—or at least the closest thing we had to one in *our* family.

Momma, on the other hand, had to really work hard to even be mistaken for a lady.

There were times, when she came to a PTA meeting or when someone died and she went to Evans Funeral Parlor, that Momma could look really pretty and act altogether nice. She had a two-piece serge suit that she wore with some black high-heeled, pointy-toe shoes and a black purse that matched. Aunt Doris said the suit fit Momma like a glove, but it was just too bad that "the blessed thing is fire-engine red." I thought the deep red was perfect for Momma.

Momma smoked Lucky Strikes; she cussed sometimes, and in the late heat of a July Fourth or Labor Day afternoon, she would drink a cold Budweiser straight out of the can. She wore shorts in the summer and slacks in the winter, and it didn't bother her one bit to put on one of Daddy's old cotton shirts that she had washed and ironed. The only jewelry Momma wore was her tiny, gold wedding-ring set and some clip-on, pearl earbobs whenever she wore the red suit.

Mostly, Momma was just clean and plain, and that was fine, but I knew Momma was no lady. She never tired of telling certain people to kiss her ass—something I was fairly sure had never come out of Grammie's or Aunt Doris's mouth.

And besides, no lady would ever get in a yellin' match with Hoyt Stevens and win, like Momma did. If Daddy yelled about something, Momma made it her business to yell back a little louder. As big a man as my Daddy was, there would be Momma, stretching to reach all of her five feet, two inches, right up in his face, giving him tit for tat and then some. She never backed down, and all he could do, short of poppin' her one, was grab his jacket and keys and storm out the door. He never hit her, but all the times he looked like he really wanted to, she always yelled the same thing at him: "Yeah...and if you ever do hit me, you long-legged bastard, you damn well better kill me!"

But by then he was usually out the door, hopping behind the wheel of his slick black '58 Ford Fairlane, headed for the Cozy Corner. The big chrome mufflers on that car would rumble as he drove away, tearing down 16th Street.

No, Momma was no lady, but Daddy was certainly no gentleman either, so that made them even.

I remember coming through the back door after school one afternoon, when Momma was on the phone. She shushed me--- and pointed me back outside, where I sat down on the back stoop outside our tiny screen porch. Maybe she thought I couldn't hear, but I could, and I quickly realized that she was on the phone with old Mr. Phelps, who managed all the mill-village houses.

From what I could figure out, Momma was telling him that she had found a used clothes dryer for thirty-five dollars, which she intended to put out on the screen porch, and the appliance man had told her that she needed a special electric plug to run a clothes dryer. Mr. Phelps must have told her that our monthly rent didn't cover such costs and, besides, if they put the plug in for her, everybody in the village would be wanting one.

After a few more minutes of arguing with old man Phelps, I heard my momma say, loud and clear but just as slowly and deliberately as you'd want.

"Everett Phelps...you can just *kiss my ass*," and with that she slammed the phone down.

We never got the clothes dryer.

And Everett Phelps never—for the rest of his natural life—had any more of my grandmother's fig preserves. Every Sunday after church for years, he'd tell Grammie how much he "sure would love to have a taste again of those heavenly figs of yours." Grammie would just look him straight in the face, smile sweetly, and never say a word.

For one simple electrical outlet, old man Phelps did himself out of one of Grantville's true delicacies—forever—and who knows whether the old coot ever made the connection. Now there's a fool.

Mr. Phelps was just one example.

Momma never hesitated to give anybody what for, even if they just so much as came near to needing it. If the bottom two pork chops in a package were fat and tough, back they went to Mr. Murray.

"Kevin, you can pull that bullshit with somebody else, but don't even try it with me," she'd say, as if Mr. Murray had purposely packed, marked, and sold that particular package of pork chops to Arlene Stevens.

If something said "preshrunk" on the label and it drew- up when Momma washed it, sales receipt or not, she returned it and got her money back. Never mind that Momma probably washed the thing in water hotter than a river just east of hell's corner—she took it back and harangued the store for selling "such junk." She said the store could "eat it" better than we could.

Momma seemed to have the idea that everybody in the world would spit on you if you were dumb enough to stand still for it. She figured it was much better to let people know right up front that if they messed with her, she could—and would—spit with the best of them. Sometimes I guess that worked, but I imagine there were other times when it didn't work at all and people just walked away, wondering what the devil had made Arlene Stevens such an angry woman.

I never knew what made Momma so angry either, but I can tell you this: the woman ran on anger. Her anger gave her the kind of energy and determination that most people never have. Other mill kids' mothers might have sat and watched TV soap stories or stood for hours out in the yard gossiping, but not my momma. We probably had the cleanest house, and the only ironed gym socks in the neighborhood, because my momma had to move—or explode. It was one or the other.

Both Grammie Stevens and Aunt Doris said my momma could run circles around most of the women they knew. I guess that's what the buzz saw of anger can do.

❧

In late 1962 Trinity Presbyterian on Hackberry and 11th Street came into some big money.

"Don't ask me how, because I know for sure some of them ain't exactly livin' at the foot of the cross," Grammie commented.

It came out in the newspaper that the old white wooden church, with the crooked steeple, was going to be torn down and replaced with a fine, new white-brick sanctuary, with an elegant copper steeple and a spacious education building right next door—all paid for by a "generous endowment."

All of Grantville buzzed, trying to figure out who had died and left Trinity a fortune, but we never heard for sure.

The Presbyterians announced they were having a huge spring rummage sale; everything had to go: pews, folding chairs, choir robes, hymnals, and, of course, two pianos. They gave two colored preachers from a small church way out in the county dibs on everything for a rock-bottom bid; they made a haul and were proud to get it. But the colored churches didn't need either of the pianos.

The older of the two pianos was an upright, and the Presbyterians wanted seventy-five dollars for it. Aunt Doris heard about it and told Grammie that it would be perfect for me but that Arlene would likely catch hell, since "Hoyt says he ain't interested in listening to a bunch of pingin' and bangin' every evening."

That may have been the case, but Grammie and Aunt Doris had spent two whole grown-up lifetimes dealing with Stevens men. They looked into each other's eyes—clearly thinking the same thing—and sat down together at Grammie's kitchen table. That's where the plan was hatched.

I'm still not sure how it all came together; all I know to tell you is what happened to me on that Tuesday afternoon in April. I was still just a child, but it made me see, clear as day, what plain, simple women can do when they make up their minds. That day I learned that men— especially the ones who act like selfish, little tyrants—can be outsmarted and pushed right out of the way, and most of the time they don't even have sense enough to realize it.

I saw that day that my daddy—the big, bad Billy Hoyt Stevens—was absolutely, undoubtedly, no match for his momma, his sister, and his wife. Those three? Now *they* were a team, I'm here to tell you. And for the rest of my life, I knew that as long as I had them on my side, I could probably do anything.

By that Tuesday, the last week in April, it was hot every day by early afternoon. We had an unusually early spring, and the dogwood and aza-leas were past their full bloom, and people were already talking about how bad the summer was going to be if April was already this hot.

On Tuesdays the sixth grade got to stay outside for an extra twenty minutes, so by the time we arrived in the library at one forty-five, we were all sweating, huffing, and puffing from our kickball showdown. Miss Evans told the boys to sit down while we girls made our read-ing choices, and I immediately picked out the new *National Geographic* magazine. I had just sat down when the eighth-grade runner from the office came through the door and handed Miss Evans a note.

I barely even looked up from my magazine, but before I knew it, Miss Evans touched my shoulder.

"Grace, get your books and your lunch box...you have to go to the office."

The room fell silent; what could it be? Was I in trouble? Was someone dead? Had Wesley been hurt? Had our house burned down? For a few seconds, I just sat there.

"Grace?...Grace, go ahead now, honey," Miss Evans said quietly.

I glanced at the teacher's face and then began to move, gathering my stuff; I felt everyone's eyes on me. Miss Evans told the class to get-on with their business as I pushed open the classroom door and then bolted down the hall.

My heart was already pounding as I took the steps two and three at a time to get down to the office on the main floor.

"Your momma called, Grace...you need to go straight to your granny's house," Mrs. Littlepage explained. The sign-out sheet was right on the counter near her desk, and with a worried look on her face, she walked over while I scribbled my name. Like me, Mrs. Littlepage knew that for me to be summoned from school like this was so unusual that something terrible—just awful—had to have happened.

"Grace, honey...let us know if there's anything we can do."

"Yes, ma'am," I said, grabbing my books off the counter and busting back out the office door. I ran by the first-grade class down in the basement and stopped long enough to see Wesley sitting in his reading group. Whatever it was, it wasn't about him, I figured. Then I darted down the hall and took the back door out of the lunch room; that would save me half a block in getting to Grammie's.

It felt strange to be the only kid on the sidewalk, but I was in such a frantic hurry I didn't give it much thought. I listened for sirens or something—*anything*—that might give me an idea of what had happened. Rounding the corner near Hargrove's grocery, I nearly knocked old Mrs. Vines down. Apologizing, I kept going, focused toward Grammie's house, just up the street now. From there I could see there were no fire trucks or ambulances, no police cars, no unfamiliar anything.

Running as fast as I could, I jumped the three front steps, dropped my books and lunch box by the old porch swing, jerked open the flimsy screen door, and stopped in the hallway. There was no unusual noise; the house was quiet, but I heard low voices coming from the living room. I braced myself and walked toward the living-room door.

For the rest of my life—of course I didn't know it right then—but truly, for the rest of my life, I would hold the image I saw next in my mind forever.

There, in that little, crowded parlor, shoved over in the back corner, partially blocking the side window, was the ugliest piano in the whole world, and around it were my momma, my aunt, and my grandmother.

I froze. Huffing and puffing from my dash to get there, I could literally feel my heart thudding against my chest, but suddenly I knew it would have been hammering away anyway. A *piano* was sitting in the living room of my grandmother's house.

Momma was down on her hands and knees, cleaning around the base and the pedals of the piano; my aunt was standing nearby with her hands on her hips, grinning like the butcher's dog; and next to her, on the rickety, old piano stool, sat my grandmother, all smiles, too.

"Well...what do you think, Grace?" my aunt Doris called to me, beaming and stepping aside. "It's all *yours*."

I couldn't speak or move; I just stood there, slack-jawed.

It was a big, old, upright *monster* of a piano, which someone had painted the most horrible, fleshy, yucky pink color I had ever seen. Most of that hideous paint was either faded or cracked. There was nothing really white about the keyboard; the notes were discolored, yellowish, and chipped, and the desk easel had been ripped away from where a music book would normally rest. It was ugly, but had my aunt just said what I thought she'd said? "It's all yours..."

That piano was mine? The earth shifted on its axis—a *piano* was sitting in my grandmother's parlor, and it was all mine.

5

Bertie El returned from a three-week Mediterranean cruise in late August that summer, claiming that travel just nearly exhausted her altogether and that she might not be able to resume teaching piano.

But by the time Labor Day passed and school began, she had recovered enough to give a two-hour talk about her trip to the Garden Club, which was written up in the newspaper. Soon she was back at it with her piano students. Unfortunately, my name was on a waiting list.

Grammie wasn't a bit discouraged.

"Oh, you mark my words; one of those O'Brien boys will quit within a month, and then, Grace Stevens, *you* will start your music lessons," she declared with confidence. Mr. O'Brien was the high-school principal, and Mrs. O'Brien had insisted that all three of their boys take piano, but everybody knew that wouldn't last.

I had spent the summer banging away on my piano, sometimes for so long that Aunt Doris would offer to buy me and Wesley an ice-cream cone from Hargrove's just to get me to stop for a while. But Grammie never minded my banging. In fact, I bet I played "Beulah Land" for her at least a half dozen times every day. It took me a while to get the whole thing down, but when I did, Grammie was thrilled. *"Beulah land, sweet Beulah land, there my home shall be eternal."* Grammie knew all the words by heart.

There was now a quart-size canning jar kept up in the kitchen cabinet over the stove at Grammie's, and I noticed that she and Aunt Doris and Momma were all often getting it down and adding coins to it. It seemed that every dime, every nickel, and even every penny that was found anywhere went in that jar—a dime from the sofa cushions, seven cents left from the milkman—it went in the jar.

And it was then, too, that three or four times a week, Daddy would say that he was missing some change from the top of the dresser, where he always put his wallet and keys. He accused Wesley of swipin' it, but Momma told him right fast that it wasn't Wesley and that she probably took it for the paper boy or the post office or what have you.

By the end of summer, the jar in Grammie's kitchen cabinet began to hold some serious money, even quarters and fifty-cent pieces.

Grammie was right, and she was wrong. Not just one of the O'Brien boys quit—they *all* did, but it took more than a month, and we heard it broke Mrs. O'Brien's heart.

"Now there's money throwed right-straight down a rathole," Grammie said, knowing full well that those O'Brien boys needed piano lessons like a hog needs a saddle.

It took until the middle of October for Mrs. Hewitt to call my aunt Doris and ask if "your niece would still like to have lessons with me?" Aunt Doris, determined not to fall all over herself with glee or gratitude, told Mrs. Hewitt coolly that she was almost certain I would be available to take that four fifteen slot on Thursdays, which was Mrs. Hewitt's last teaching appointment of the week. Aunt Doris said she would let Mrs. Hewitt know for sure the next day.

The cost, it seemed, was a whoppin' twelve dollars a month, which did not include the sheet music and workbooks for all beginning students. When Aunt Doris called back Mrs. Hewitt made it clear that she was not interested in hearing how Doris's niece already played by ear; she assured my aunt that I would most likely have to be "untrained then retrained properly," which meant I *would* be a beginner.

That evening, at Grammie's kitchen table, the jar of coins was emptied. I counted pennies, Grammie counted dimes and nickels, and Momma counted quarters and half-dollars, while Aunt Doris kept the tally. Altogether there was $21. 58, which was enough for one whole month, part of the next month, and hopefully enough to pay for the first music books. I was amazed.

"Now...I think...just to simplify things...we ought to just keep all this to ourselves," Aunt Doris suggested, looking straight at me.

Momma knew I'd probably be poppin' at the gills to tell *everybody*, so she jumped right to the point.

"Grace, here's the deal—the less your daddy knows about this, the better. Do you understand?"

I looked at her, a bit confused.

"You know how he is, Grace...he didn't like it back in the spring when I threw-in twenty-five dollars toward the piano, so he sure ain't gonna stand still for this if he finds out," Momma said, lighting a Lucky Strike.

Grammie reached over and patted my hands.

"Honey, there's just some things that men are better off kept out of...it just makes it easier for everybody. So you just go right on and start your music lessons next week, and don't worry about a thing. Wesley can stay here with me, and when Doris gets home from work, she can get y'all home. We'll just tell your daddy that from now on Thursdays will be your day to come to Grammie's," she explained gently.

Momma couldn't resist.

"And that will suit the long-legged horse's ass just fine, since then he can go straight on to the Spotlight when he leaves work," she said, plucking a bit of tobacco off her tongue.

Aunt Doris finished putting all the change in two envelopes.

"I'll take this by the bank tomorrow and get some bills." She picked up the empty jar and walked toward the cabinet. "And this is going right back up here for more change."

It was all set. Next Thursday I was going to walk up the hill to the big stone house, walk right through that wide front door, sit down at that big black piano, and start my music lessons.

Nothing—nothing at all—seemed impossible to me right then.

Snivelin' and cryin', that's what Momma called it.

For as long as I could remember, Momma would say, "Stop that snivelin' and cryin'!" anytime something happened, because she said she couldn't stand a kid squallin'. As a result, neither I nor Wesley ever cried much, at least certainly not in front of her. So I guess you could say it was a good thing that the first evening I walked out of Mrs. Hewitt's piano studio Momma was workin' late at the Buddy Burger.

Needless to say, I had *not* walked through that big front door, and I had *not* sat down at that grand piano. Thanks to the gardener, who saw me headed up the front steps, I was quickly herded around to the little path at the side of the house, where I met Susie Ackerman, who had just finished her lesson.

Susie spoke to me, and I must have responded, but I really don't remember. I was focused...no, the truth is I was scared and worried, because something told me that things were about to change and that there wouldn't be any goin' back. Just how I knew that is still a mystery to me, but I knew it, and I was right.

Lord, was I right.

The first thing Mrs. Hewitt did was look at my hands, and thank goodness Grammie had made me wash my face and hands and straighten out my ponytail before I left her house.

Once my hands passed inspection, I sat down on the piano stool, and Mrs. Hewitt sat down in a chair right beside me. She told me to play something for her, anything I'd like. She sat there and didn't say a word; she just watched and listened while I pounded out "Onward Christian Soldiers."

I did my dead-dog, bull's eye best, I tell you, applying every little piece of my piano game that I had honed now for nearly four years. I used every trick, every little twist I knew, and when I finished, I felt pretty proud of myself. I figured it was more than she had heard from Susie Ackerman for sure.

After a long silence, I finally looked at Mrs. Hewitt. She took a deep breath and sighed; then she sat back in her chair and looked at me.

"Grace, who taught you to play like that?"

I was eager and pleased to answer.

"Oh, nobody...I just watched people play and made a game out of the keys..."

She frowned.

"What kind of game?"

"Well, first I started noticin' threes"—I played three notes with a spare in between each of them as she watched—"and I called them sets. Then I started seein' that the sets could be used to make a path..." I started playing other "sets" for her, mostly on the white keys. She never said a word; she just listened and watched me as I did my best to explain this game of mine.

Maybe I wasn't doing a very good job, or maybe Mrs. Hewitt had heard enough, but after about five minutes, she stopped me.

"I see," she said and reached over to touch my hands, nudging them off the keys and into my lap. Then she pushed her chair back and crossed her legs.

"Grace, turn around this way...toward me...and let's talk," Mrs. Hewitt said, and that's what we did for the rest of my first music lesson.

The things Mrs. Hewitt said to me scared me, excited me, embarrassed me, hurt me, and shocked me. I walked out of that studio into the crisp October twilight, and as soon as I got far enough down the hill and out of sight of her house, I sat down on the curb beneath one of the big elms and I cried. And I didn't just snivel; I sobbed.

I pulled my skirt over my knees, put my head down into the pleats, and I cried as long and as hard as I think I ever had. I was nearly twelve years old, but I sure didn't feel like it.

Finally I heard the dinner whistle blow for the second shift down at the mill; it was five thirty. I stopped crying and wiped my eyes with my sweater sleeve; then I stood-up and started on down the hill. Somewhere deep in my head, I heard the echo of my daddy's words about pianos and music lessons and such—*who did I think I was anyway?*

When I walked through the back door at Grammie's that Thursday evening after my first music lesson, it was plain that something was really wrong. My nose and eyes were red and puffy, and when I saw the eager, expectant look on Grammie's face, it started all over again as tears welled- up in my eyes. I was just so glad Momma was still at work.

"Wesley, go to the living room and watch *Lassie*...it's comin' on in just a few minutes," Aunt Doris suggested, gently guiding Wesley out of the kitchen.

"And close the door, buddy," she called after him.

I sat at the kitchen table--blubbering away--and told them *everything* Mrs. Hewitt had said to me. Ten minutes later, Grammie and Aunt Doris looked at each. I think they knew right then that it just wouldn't do for Momma to ever hear some of *those* details.

Aunt Doris said Mrs. Hewitt, as a Christian woman, could have gone a long time without making some of the comments she'd made to me but that it was now in everybody's best interest that my momma never know. Otherwise the fat would hit the fire for sure.

"That's about all we'd need...yo' Momma arrested for slappin' Bertie El Hewitt into the middle of next week," my aunt said as she handed me a cold, wet wash cloth for my face.

Grammie put a tall glass of iced tea in front of me.

"Well, honey..., you just stop cryin' now...that old biddy can keep that twelve dollars. You don't have to go back... just quit right now," she said.

The word "quit" barely got past Grammie's lips before Aunt Doris whirled around, and basically squared-up on her own momma.

"Quit!?" Aunt Doris almost bellowed, and then repeated herself. "*Quit?*"

Looking Grammie straight in the face and shaking her finger over at me, my aunt held forth.

"She'll quit over my dead body! She's not quittin'..."

Aunt Doris then leaned over the table and looked hard at me.

"Do you understand me, Grace? You are *not* quittin'. I'll be *damned* if we'll let Miss Uppity-Snobnose-I'm-Better-Than-Everybody-Hewitt make you quit before you even get started...so just get that idea out of your head..." --Aunt Doris then turned toward Grammie again-- "and that goes for you, too, Momma."

Grammie and I looked at each. Doris Stevens saying she was "damned" about anything was a first as far as I knew, so she was really serious. I never even got to say that I wouldn't have quit anyway, no matter what. But what Mrs. Hewitt had said to me was scorching.

⁓০

Mrs. Hewitt had told me that I obviously had some talent for music, talent that might be developed into something if I was willing to really work hard. She said that the piano, "a magnificent instrument," required patience and commitment and long years of study and that no one--living or dead---"has had ever totally mastered the piano." A true pianist, she explained, never pounded or banged out a note but brought sounds and vibrations alive with finesse and feeling so that the piano actually "sang."

"Almost anybody can sit down and hammer out 'Amazing Grace...' or something ridiculous like that 'Alley Cat' song from the radio," Mrs. Hewitt said, "but it takes a true musician-----a devoted student who knows the piano-----to actually be a pianist."

She asked me what I wanted, because, she said, if I didn't really want to be a pianist, I could just go on doing what I'd been doing.

"But" —she leaned back again in her chair, — "if you want to study piano with me, you have to start over."

For the next twenty minutes, Mrs. Hewitt talked and talked, and I listened.

She told me that I had to completely forget my game; I had to wipe it out of my mind and never again let myself play a piano, for any reason, using that game. I had to let go of every tune, every song, I had ever managed to pick-out by ear and start over *completely* with the rock-bottom basics of the piano. I had to learn correct fingering, I had to learn scales and chords and theory, and I had to learn the classics—none of which could happen until I did away with my game.

I sat there listening to every word she said. Then I began to wonder how I could do that; how could I wipe my game out of my mind? And how could I never again sit down at my big, ugly piano in Grammie's living room and play "Beulah Land" for her? My piano game was old; it had been with me a long time, and I wasn't sure I could even *make* myself forget it.

"So, Grace..., if you want to study piano with me, you must promise to put an end, once and for all, to your game and to only play the music I teach you," she said.

I just sat there, probably looking dumb and lost, which was not what Mrs. Hewitt wanted, I guess.

Maybe she thought that I totally understood and grasped what she was saying, and that I should gratefully jump-up with delight and fall at her feet for the exceptional opportunity she was offering me, I don't know. But I didn't do that.

I didn't do anything. And Mrs. Hewitt evidently did not *like* that I didn't do anything.

After a long pause, and without leaving her chair, without raising her voice, and without so much as taking a breath, she laid into me. It wasn't until she finished, minutes later, that I actually said anything.

Mrs. Hewitt said that she wasn't a bit surprised, and that children like me, from low-class families, rarely ever took advantage of good opportunities when they had the chance. She said that what little ability any of us might ever have would just as well be flushed down the sewer. She said that anybody could plainly see-- from my run-down shoes and filthy socks, my ragged fingernails, and my clumsiness---where I came from, and that girls like me, without proper guidance and no advantages, not to even mention correct grammar, would do well to end- up just like my momma----—in some joint, "slingin' hash with a Marlboro hanging out of your mouth." She told me to just suit myself ... and go right on banging out hymns like a happy clown at the Baptist church from now "till Gabe blows his bugle" for all she cared. It was, she said, nothing to her one way or the other.

Then Mrs. Hewitt got up abruptly and walked across the little studio; she switched on another lamp, then stopped, smoothing her skirt before she glanced at her watch. She was clearly ready for me to leave.

I stood-up from the piano stool and pulled the folded envelope with twelve dollars in it out of the pocket of my skirt. I stepped over and handed it to Mrs. Hewitt; then I finally spoke.

"Yes, ma'am," I said.

There was a long silence as she just stood there, holding the envelope, with me looking straight at her. Finally she spoke.

"'Yes, ma'am.'? Is that what you said?" she asked, knowing as well as I did that that was exactly what I'd just said.

"Yes, ma'am," I repeated.

She looked at me, and I wasn't sure, but from the look on her face, she was either surprised or shocked or something.

"Yes, ma'am...I will forget my piano game ...and I do want to study the piano. I love the piano," I said quietly.

Mrs. Hewitt gasped and covered her mouth with her hand. Then she suddenly rushed out of the studio, motioning to me over her shoulder to sit back down on the stool, which I did.

Of course, it took many years for Mrs. Hewitt to later tell Aunt Doris how she lay awake that night, in her big house on Riverview, thinking about me, Grace Stevens, and how she might at last have a child with some genuine talent, a child who truly wanted to study music and who might, with Bertie El's help, actually achieve something extraordinary with it.

Tears had dampened Bertie El's satin pillowcase that night----she was so ashamed of what she had said to me. Mrs. Hewitt told Aunt Doris she still could hear how I, a child from the mill village, "had calmly and politely, with such dignity," spoken the words Bertie El had, for years, been yearning to hear from a student: "I love the piano."

6

The money Momma made working at the Buddy Burger began to make a big difference in our lives. Suddenly there were new curtains in the living room, Wesley got to join the Cub Scouts, and at least once a week, we had center-cut pork chops or a roast.

At Christmas that year, Wesley and I both got new winter coats, he got a new bicycle, and, at last, I got a big bride doll. She was too gorgeous and perfect to actually play with, but having her sit regally on my bed all the time put me right up there with most of the other girls my age. To *not* have a bride doll was pretty much the height of hopelessness, I guess.

You might have thought that Daddy would be pretty proud that there was money now for some nice little extras, but he still didn't like Momma working and not being right there at home every minute of every day. I didn't understand why he wanted her at home all the time, since he didn't stay home himself hardly at all. Daddy said that "outdoorsmen" like himself deserved to have "hobbies and pastimes," like hunting and fishing. I didn't have the nerve to point out to him that the Spotlight and the Cozy Corner weren't "outdoors" but he sure spent a lot of time at them, too.

Whenever someone would mention to Momma that they had seen Daddy's car "late last night at the Spotlight," she would get a smirky, little smile on her face and say how much she appreciated them letting her know something that she could easily "have bet her life" on in the first place.

I had this image in my head that there was a lady in a fancy red dress at the Spotlight and that my daddy went there to dance with her. I don't know why I thought that, but I could see it, clear as a bell, on the Friday and Saturday nights when Daddy didn't come home and I could hear Momma in the kitchen, smokin' her Luckies and ironing way into the night, listening to the hit parade on WSGN Radio 610.

After the holidays, it didn't take long for it to occur to Daddy that there was about ten dollars a month that seemed to be disappearing. At first Momma told him that she was a working woman and that she was not about to answer to him for every red cent she spent, but with a piano now sitting at Grammie's, big as life, he *knew* what was going on.

The twelve dollars every month for Mrs. Hewitt, plus an extra $2.65 or so for my music workbooks, comprised a small fortune to hear him tell it. There was just no end—apparently—to what he could accomplish if he didn't have a "hardheaded dumbass woman throwin' good money away on silly shit" like music lessons and Cub Scouts.

Momma pointed out to him that she was certain the owners of both the Spotlight and the Cozy Corner would somehow manage to avoid bankruptcy even if he failed to give them every extra nickel he could put his hands on.

It was an ongoing battle, and I had a feeling that it would never end.

I was relieved, though, that now Daddy knew I was taking music lessons. The pressure to keep it from him had weighed on me; plus I had been scared to death that Wesley would let it slip. It was out there now, and that was good. But there was still a secret---the secret between me and Aunt Doris and Grammie of what Mrs. Hewitt had said to me.

Aunt Doris and Grammie were on a mission.

After my first trip up the hill to Mrs. Hewitt's, they dug through every closet, every chest, every chifforobe in the house, pulling out bundle after bundle of various fabrics, some decades old, until they found what they needed—a nice navy-and-gray plaid wool and a dark green tweed. Within a week, Aunt Doris had made two jumpers for me, one of which Grammie hand-smocked.

From Miller's Discount Bin, Momma bought two white blouses with Peter Pan collars, a three pack of white cotton panties, and, to my everlasting surprise, two white cotton brassieres. Aunt Doris came in the next afternoon with a pair of black flats that fit me perfectly, plus two pairs of lovely white knee socks. I was stunned.

"Now, Grace, from now on, when you get here on Thursday afternoons, get yourself a quick bite to eat and then jump in the bathtub. These two jumpers will be kept right here in my closet with the blouses"—Aunt Doris showed me—"and you alternate wearing one, then the other, each week. Understand, hon?"

"Yes, ma'am," I said, watching her place my new shoes and knee socks up on the closet shelf.

"And always put on clean undergarments, and Grammie will help you with your hair...and, oh, don't forget to brush your teeth, too," she added. Aunt Doris said she was disappointed that I didn't have a blazer, but, by gosh, I'd have one soon.

My momma, my aunt, and my grandmother were evidently out to give Mrs. Hewitt a run for her money, which was fine with me. And in addition to my new music-lesson clothes, something else happened that I couldn't believe.

On Wednesday night, before I returned to Mrs. Hewitt's studio for my second lesson, Aunt Doris's friend Dedee Higgins came to Grammie's house and gave me a manicure. Yep, that's right—a *real* manicure.

While Wesley watched *Tarzan* in the living room, there we were, all seated around the kitchen table, Momma smokin' Luckies, Grammie thumbing through the *Reader's Digest*, Aunt Doris knitting, and me with my hands spread out on a clean dish towel while Dedee worked away on my fingernails. It was amazing, and from then on, at least once a month, Dedee worked her magic. My nails were clean and short, covered in clear polish, and I was told that they had to stay that way. They did.

Who knew that taking music lessons could lead to such a transformation? It was exciting to say the least, but I knew that all hell and then some would break loose if my daddy ever heard about all this.

Little did he know that a whole operation, a fine-tuned, detailed production was underway right under his nose, so that every Thursday afternoon, while he sat on a barstool, smokin' and jokin', his *own* momma and sister were in cahoots with his *own* wife, making it possible for his *own* daughter to do something that he said was silly and uncalled for.

Sometimes I almost laughed out loud just thinking about it.

Later on I could look back and see that in six short months an avalanche of changes tumbled over me, changes I really had no choice about. I grew taller and lankier almost overnight, according to Momma, and everything from my lips to my feet grew and filled out. By late spring, everything I owned either had to be altered or thrown out, which kept Aunt Doris busy for weeks. Sadly the new winter coat I had gotten for Christmas now looked like it belonged to someone else—someone with arms much shorter than mine.

And, of course, my music lessons changed everything.

It was hard for some people to accept that I wouldn't play the piano at school or at church anymore like I used to do. And Grammie, still wanted me to play "Beulah Land" for her, but I kept my promise to Mrs. Hewitt. No one could understand why I wouldn't play now that I was actually taking music lessons. There was more to it than I felt like I could explain, so I didn't bother. I had confidence that at some point I would again sit down at a piano and play but that, unlike before, I would *know* the music.

I rarely played outside anymore. The things that had once been the center of my childhood—bikes, skates, street ball—no longer interested me. Except for being outside to keep an eye on Wesley sometimes, I was inside, either at my piano at Grammie's or at the kitchen table in our house.

Back in late October, Mrs. Hewitt's only reaction to the "new" Grace Stevens had been a big, warm smile and an approving nod of her head. I showed up every Thursday in my white blouses and jumpers and clean knee socks, with my long, manicured fingers and my neat ponytail. At first I felt as if I was going to church, but then I got used to it. I was probably the best-dressed, cleanest student Mrs. Hewitt could ever hope to have, and believe it or not, the key word there was "student."

Every day—every single day, I'm sayin'—I worked on my music.

At first the only things I was allowed to actually play were my Hanon exercises; again and again I went up the keyboard and then back down the keyboard, using the exact fingering of each exercise. It was slow-going at the start, but as my fingers got stronger and more agile, I could move right along. I did page after page of Hanon, as my fingers seemed to take on an accurate, precise life of their own at the keyboard.

Then I did my music workbooks. I wrote and studied scale after scale, line after line, of all the basic major and minor keys. I learned about meters, measures, and rhythms. I learned sharps and flats, I learned chords, I learned fifths and thirds, and I learned the silent language of music symbols and notations. It was all absolutely amazing to me, and slowly, after only a few months, it all began to fit together so beautifully that it almost took my breath away at times. I loved every bit of it.

Suddenly, the fact that I could no longer play "Last Date" or "Beulah Land" didn't matter so much anymore. Instead, I felt as if I was learning something so magical, so unbelievably perfect, that songs like those were only the very fringe of what was possible.

Thanks to the jar of money in Grammie's kitchen cabinet, by summer my big, ugly piano had been tuned and a metronome was purchased for me. Aunt Doris found an old pharmacy lamp at a garage sale, and it was placed on top of the ugly upright, with its head hanging over to shine right down on me and my Hanon.

I was at the piano so much that Grammie finally moved her little black-and-white television out of the living room and placed it on the dresser in her bedroom. Nothing and no one interfered with my music.

Then I arrived at Mrs. Hewitt's one Thursday afternoon, and from a brown wrapper, she placed four classical piano collections in front of me: Beethoven, Bach, Schubert, and Clementi. All my hours of workbooks and exercises started to fall into place, and a whole new world began for me that day.

The first time I played through a simple sonatina, able to read and understand the notes, the register, the accents—everything on the page before me—I knew I'd found myself. Suddenly no hymns at Mount Vernon Baptist, no boogie-woogie ditties, or radio pop hits meant anything to me. My old game was dead and gone, and in its place was a new, true yearning tinted with a desperate hope that I could—somehow, someway—make the piano my life.

I think it was the fall I'd started ninth grade at Grantville Central High School, that Mrs. Hewitt had called my aunt Doris and asked if it might not be possible for me to start visiting with her on Sunday evenings for the purpose of "exposing Grace to some classical pianists" by way of her "new stereophonic record player."

When Aunt Doris told Momma about the offer, the first thing Momma asked me was how I felt about missing church on Sunday nights, since that was when the Baptist Youth Group always socialized. It was no contest for me.

So at about five o'clock every Sunday evening, I got back into my church clothes and walked up the hill to Mrs. Hewitt's, and believe it or not, I actually walked up the front steps and right through that big, fine front door, right past that glossy black piano.

Mrs. Hewitt's help was not there on Sunday evenings, but a light supper was always left for us, which we ate out in the sun -room. We had chicken salad, or pimento cheese, or club sandwiches, with fresh fruit and buttermilk pie, on the most beautiful, little china plates I had ever seen. They were so fine and thin I think you could probably have read a newspaper through them, and we ate with ornate, silver forks that would have put Aunt Doris's Biddle teaspoons in the shade, let me tell you. We used white napkins, with Mrs. Hewitt's initials on them, and drank iced tea from heavy glasses that she said had come from Ireland.

Mrs. Hewitt's new stereo was a major piece of furniture made of dark wood, which took- up almost one whole wall of her sun-room, especially since she had ordered a new "étagère," as she called it, built beside it to hold her LPs—---- long-playing stereo records, she said. So there, on Sunday nights, I learned a lot.

Names like Clara Haskil, Van Cliburn, and Myra Hess became my favorites, as they played Chopin, Mozart, and Rachmaninoff. I had never heard anything so wonderful.

Sometimes Mrs. Hewitt would explain to me what I was about to hear and what I should be listening for ; then other times she would wait and ask me afterwards what I had heard or recognized and how it made me feel.

Those three hours on Sunday evenings absolutely flew by to me. The sounds from that stereo would stay with me for hours and hours, sometimes even echoing into my dreams for the next few nights.

One Sunday night I was following Mrs. Hewitt out of the sun-room, through the dining room, toward the foyer and the front door, when I reached out quickly, bravely, and touched her magnificent grand piano.

She had already commented, weeks earlier, on how I so often stopped and looked at that piano.

"Grace, that piano is a custom-made instrument ...worth thousands of dollars. The soundboard is Sitka spruce, the keys are solid ivory, and the case is made of the rarest African ebony from Mozambique. It is *not*, my dear, a practice piano," she'd said almost sternly, walking on toward the sun-room.

But I managed to touch it that one time, and she didn't even see me do it.

It did not occur to me until later that my Sunday evenings with Mrs. Hewitt were perhaps her way, intentionally or not, of protecting me from the minefield that was high school. Even without kids of her own, maybe she just somehow knew that for those of us who weren't destined to be cheerleaders or homecoming queens or star athletes, there had to be a concerted effort----some hard evidence—to show us that there were other worthy things to do. After all, almost every one of her piano students quit their music lessons somewhere between eighth and tenth grade.

But that never crossed my mind; no boyfriend, no club, or social clique came close to my interest in piano. And Mrs. Hewitt, whether she meant to or not, saw to it that my passion did not wane.

Eighteen months —that's how long it took my daddy to figure out that I was no longer going to church on Sunday nights. Why it mattered to him, one way or another, that I was being given some special attention from Mrs. Hewitt never made sense to me or Momma. He ranted and raved about it to Grammie and Aunt Doris, saying that I was going to end-up "thinkin' too much" of myself and that for riding so high, I was bound to "take a bad fall." He said over and over that "Arlene is a stupid fool...a regular fruit cake...without a lick of common sense about raisin' kids."

Aunt Doris calmly recommended that he just shut-up and have another Pabst Blue Ribbon which I'm sure he did.

⌁

Daddy left on a Tuesday in April, just before I finished tenth grade.

Two days earlier, on a Sunday afternoon of all times, Momma and him had a wing-ding, ripsnorter of a brawl. Evidently it had been brewin' for some time, because from what I heard, as Wesley and I hustled out the back door to walk the four blocks to Grammie's, there were several different issues.

There was my spending too much time at Mrs. Hewitt's house. There was Wesley being allowed to go to boy-scout camp after making another D in language. There was Momma now being manager of the Buddy Burger, and there was Aunt Doris and Momma finding a used spinet piano that they wanted to buy for me, so the pink monster at Grammie's could be laid to rest.

All of this, evidently, did not suit Daddy; he wanted to buy a new rod and reel to use in a three-day bass-fishing tournament that cost fifty dollars just to sign up and another hundred dollars to rent a rig for him and his friend Pete to use. Evidently Momma had the gumption to ask him what exactly would be the return value in him blowing two hundred dollars, three days, and no telling how much beer money attempting to catch a fish that might—or might not---even be fittin' to eat? That was too much for him, I guess.

Who knows what the final blow was or who struck it. All Wesley and I knew was that things were unusually quiet Monday evening. Daddy hadn't gone to work that day; he wasn't home, and he never came home that night. Momma ironed.

Then on Tuesday afternoon, I came in the front door about the same time Wesley walked in through the back porch, and there sat Momma at the kitchen table, smoking a Lucky. It was 3:20, and she had on her Buddy Burger uniform. On the kitchen floor lay the wooden shelf where she had kept her little collection of blue-and-white dishes that she liked so much, and every last one of them was smashed to bits. She didn't seem upset, but she was very quiet as she told us to sit down.

Taking a long draw on her Lucky, Momma looked at me and then at Wesley.

"Your daddy's gone. He got fired from his job this mornin', and he's gone—took his clothes and his guns and all his fishin' shit...and the car," she said.

Wesley kind of gasped and looked at me, but I didn't say anything and kept my eyes on Momma.

"Well, where'd he go, Momma?" my brother asked.

"I don't know, Wes...said he was gettin' the hell out of Tennessee and away from me—that's all." She propped her Lucky in the ashtray on the table then rested her elbows on the edge.

"He told your aunt Doris and your granny that he's goin' to Mobile... said there's plenty of work down there on the docks, so we'll see. But the main thing is that we'll be OK...do you understand me?"

She said it as about half a question and half a fact. We stared at her, and then she said it again.

"We'll be OK...and that's what matters most, right?"

Almost in unison, Wesley and I answered her. "Yes, ma'am."

Momma got up and called her friend Polly, who came to drive her back to the Buddy Burger, and she told me, as she went out the door, not to touch the broken dishes.

I made fish sticks and macaroni for me and Wesley that night. The shelf and all the broken blue-and-white dishes lay right there, untouched, for nearly a week, until late one night I heard Momma sweeping it all up. She never said what happened, but I knew, just as sure as I'm standing here, what Daddy had done.

Mill families had thirty days to vacate a company house once an employee was terminated, but Momma told Mr. Phelps that she'd move when she found what she could afford and that if he didn't like it, he could take her to court. Then she told him to kiss her ass... and hung up.

On the last Sunday in May, I played in my third piano recital.

It was held in the chapel of Mrs. Hewitt's church, and afterward there was cake and punch in the church library. By then I was the last of Mrs. Hewitt's students to perform, and that afternoon I wore a beautiful pastel-pink sundress with spaghetti straps that Aunt Doris had made. Grammie beaded the bodice with tiny, white fake pearls. I wore matching pink shoes, with princess heels, and sheer beige nylons. My hair was pinned up in a French twist, and I wore Aunt Doris's ivory rose earrings.

Having practiced a few times on the baby grand piano in the Episcopal church, I felt comfortable as I sat down that afternoon to play. As Mrs. Hewitt had taught me, I took a few seconds to compose myself and relax before lifting my hands off my lap to touch the keyboard. I noticed how nice the full skirt of my dress looked, falling gently over the piano bench, and then for some reason, it suddenly crossed my mind that my daddy was probably never going to see me play the piano. He had not come to my first two recitals, and now he was gone, probably for good. That was really sad to me.

Then I glanced over to the third pew on the right, and there sat Momma, Aunt Doris, and Grammie, their eyes focused, earnestly, on me. Behind them I could see Wesley sitting with the Reed girl and her brother.

The people who mattered most to me were all right there, and *what* mattered most to me was also right there in front of me—a fine piano, waiting for me to connect myself to it. A second later, my hands touched the keys, and for the next six and a half minutes, time was suspended. I played the first movement of Beethoven's *Moonlight* Sonata without so much as a single snag.

The next thing I knew, the audience was standing and applauding. There were no shouts or cheers, no whistles, just a solid, steady applause that went on until I finally stood up from the piano and slowly bowed. I saw tears in Grammie's eyes, and I saw that Mrs. Hewitt, standing and clapping too, was staring at me with a look on her face I had never seen.

Later on, she told Aunt Doris that she knew right then that I could compete in the statewide Teachers' Piano Competition held every year in Knoxville at the University of Tennessee and that she was going to see that I did.

"No one in Grantville even knows what that is," Aunt Doris assured her.

"Well, they will, Doris," she answered. "Believe you me, they will."

Two weeks later, we moved into a nice, little garage apartment just across the street from Grammie's house. It belonged to Mrs. Adair and had been built ten years earlier for old Mrs. Adair, who had since died. Momma scrubbed the place up one side and down the other; then we painted all the walls a nice, warm beige. She and I shared twin beds in the only bedroom, and she bought a new fold-out sofa for Wesley to sleep on in the living room. Everything else that wouldn't fit in was either given to the Goodwill or stuffed into Grammie's old garage.

There was no more mention of a better piano for me. Momma needed a car, and once we were moved and settled in, she bought a used Corvair from Big-Hearted Eddie, a used-car shyster out on 119, near the Buddy Burger. Apparently he really liked Momma and gave her a good deal.

That summer I went to work three afternoons a week at the Kress store. Everything I earned went to three simple things: lipstick, panty hose, and music books.

The only problem was Wesley.

It was after Daddy left and we moved into the garage apartment that Wesley changed. He ended up passing fifth grade only with the under-standing that he'd do summer school for six weeks of language arts, which cost Momma thirty-five dollars. She made him cut grass and earn part of it, but then it fell to me and Grammie to get him up every morn-ing and out the door to class.

He quit boy scouts, saying he didn't care about it anymore, and then he started refusing to go to church, saying that he shouldn't have to go since I didn't go every week anymore. He had a point about that, but Momma still made him go.

Maybe it was because I was working at my first job that summer, or maybe it was because Wesley needed some extra attention or some-thing, but that was when Momma and I grew further apart.

We had never been close, the way I knew other mothers and daugh-ters were, but with my piano and my little job and my manicures and my wardrobe, which Aunt Doris kept expanding and fine-tuning, Momma and I had even less in common. We were like roommates sharing that tiny garage bedroom. I spent more time with Mrs. Hewitt and with Grammie and Aunt Doris than I ever spent with Momma, but don't get me wrong—I was OK with that.

Between managing the Buddy Burger six days a week and trying to keep Wesley from going straight down the path toward a full-blown membership into juvenile delinquency, Momma had enough to do.

Of course, even a blind man could see it; with Daddy gone, Wesley was now surrounded by four women. It was plain that he had decided to become Daddy, to take Daddy's place as best he could at age eleven. Wesley got more angry and smart-mouthed by the day.

Just before school started in September, he refused again to take out the garbage, something which Momma had had enough of. Before it was over, Wesley was crying and saying he wanted to go live with Daddy, to which Momma yelled, over her shoulder on the way out the door for work, that if he could find his daddy, he was "sure welcome to take up the matter with him" for all she cared. She didn't mean that, but Wesley probably didn't know it.

Sixth grade got off to a rocky start for Wesley, while I began my junior year of high school wearing skirts that Aunt Doris claimed were "disgracefully short" but were nowhere close to what Susie Ackerman and the other cheerleaders were wearing. Aunt Doris was making most of my clothes, but I did have a couple of Villager sweaters and a John Romaine purse.

And finally, for the first time in my life that I could remember, I had no ponytail. In its place was a plain pageboy haircut that I kept teased up pretty high and plastered with hair spray. It was the style. To Grammie's undying horror, I got my ears pierced and wore tiny gold balls all the time—also the style.

Mrs. Hewitt told me in September that she had a plan for me to perform at something special during the holidays, so she had me go to work on some Christmas pieces I had never heard. Some of it was the most challenging music I had seen, and between eleventh-grade trigonometry, Liszt, and Tchaikovsky, I stayed busy all the time.

And Wesley? Well, he stayed in trouble all the time.

Momma, Aunt Doris, and Grammie were in a never-ending struggle to keep him in school and out of the principal's office.

The Sunday evenings at Mrs. Hewitt's now included another of her older piano students, Hughie Renfroe, whose dad was an accountant at the mill. Hughie was a year behind me in school, but I knew him—because everybody knew him.

Hughie was a big sissy, but I liked him. He hated sports, was president of the Latin Club, played the violin and the piano, and loved all kinds of plants and fish. The biology teacher once took Hughie's whole class to the Renfroe's house to see Hughie's forty-gallon aquarium filled with dozens of tropical fish. That was considered pretty cool, but not cool enough—Hughie was still a sissy, and nothing could overcome that.

Anyway, Hughie came to Mrs. Hewitt's, and between Mrs. Hewitt and him, I learned all kinds of things, some of which were not about music.

I learned to always keep a dinner napkin folded in half on my lap. I learned the difference between a seafood fork and a salad fork. I learned about demitasses, and I learned a whole bunch of double entendres, mostly from literature. Good manners and etiquette—Mrs. Hewitt said they were the glue of civilization, which I thought was a little exaggerated.

I figured if people ever got hungry enough, they really wouldn't care what fork they were supposed to use.

That first Christmas without Daddy was different, of course. There was no room for a Christmas tree in our little garage apartment. Momma hung our plastic wreath on the door, with a big, new red bow on it, and we hung our stockings on the kitchen windowsill. Our gifts went under the little tree at Grammie's house.

A week before Christmas, I arrived by taxi, courtesy of Mrs. Hewitt, at the front door of the Winnatoska Country Club, wearing a maroon velvet dress and low-heel black pumps. Aunt Doris had offered to drive me, but Mrs. Hewitt said no, she'd take care of it. She had also wanted me to wear a black dress—the standard for performing—but Aunt Doris said absolutely not, that I was too young to wear a black dress.

I waited outside the ballroom while the 110 ladies of the auxiliary finished their business and had dessert. Suddenly one of the double doors opened, and Mrs. Hewitt walked out. She was wearing a beautiful white wool suit with a mink collar; big gold and pearl earrings, the size of fifty-cent pieces, hung from her ears. She smiled at me, and I stood up.

"Grace, I'll introduce you in just a few minutes...then you may walk straight to the Steinway and begin. You have your music, don't you?" she asked.

"Yes, ma'am...right here." I picked it up from the glass table beside me. She always told me to bring it, whether I felt like I needed it or not.

"Fine...now do your best. I've assured these ladies that they're in for a real treat," she said, turning toward the door. She stopped suddenly and looked back at me.

"Grace, what is your full name?"

"Grace Jeanette," I said.

"Lovely," she said, nodding her head slightly, "Grace Jeanette."

"Yes, ma'am," I said as I sat back down.

Mrs. Hewitt went back into the ballroom, leaving the door open so I could hear.

For the first time, it suddenly dawned on me—I was about to play for a roomful of people, over a hundred women, none of whom I really knew. I, Grace Stevens, alone, was evidently the featured entertainment for their annual Christmas luncheon...me, just me. Luckily, I didn't have any more time to think about it—I heard Mrs. Hewitt at the microphone.

"...so please welcome my star student, a very talented young lady, Miss Grace Jeanette Stevens."

A few seconds later, I stopped beside the big Steinway and bowed slightly as the applause died away. I sat down, took a long, deep breath, as Mrs. Hewitt always said to do, and then I began. By the end of my first piece, Holst's "In the Bleak Midwinter," I was absorbed, and then it didn't matter who, or how many, was in that ball room.

⌒◯

The only person to hear from Daddy that Christmas was Wesley. On the twenty-third of December, the mailman delivered several Christmas cards to Grammie's house, and one of them was addressed to Wesley Lee Stevens. Inside was a large, glittery Christmas card, with a five-dollar bill taped to it; there was one word written at the bottom, "Dad."

As soon as possible, Momma and Aunt Doris snatched-up that envelope, but there was no return address. Other than the Mobile, Alabama, postmark, there was no way to know where Daddy was living. Not one word was spoken about that or about Daddy.

Yes, it would have been nice if Daddy had at least sent me a card, too, but truthfully, it didn't matter much to me. By then my performance at Winnatoska Country Club for the Ladies Auxiliary had brought me more attention than I could have imagined. Two photographs were on the front page of the next Sunday newspaper, one of me at the Steinway and another of me standing with Mrs. Hewitt and the Auxiliary president. The article below the pictures was mostly what Mrs. Hewitt told the newspaper about me and the music I had played at the luncheon.

Grammie bought twelve newspapers and sent the front page to everybody she knew outside of Grantville.

But being in the newspaper was just the start. After the holidays, something so unbelievable happened that at first I thought it was probably just a joke.

It began when Mrs. Hewitt called Aunt Doris one night in late January. You might think that Momma would have been slightly peeved that Mrs. Hewitt always called my aunt rather than my mother, but it didn't bother Momma at all, I guess.

Anyway, Mrs. Hewitt called and told Aunt Doris that one of the ladies at the Christmas luncheon, who'd enjoyed hearing me play, had a lovely spinet—a nice Baldwin—that she would very much like me to have. The piano was no longer being played, and the lady, a Mrs. Holderness, thought I might like to have it, especially after Mrs. Hewitt told her about my ugly, old upright. So, Mrs. Hewitt wondered, would it be all right if she arranged for a local moving crew to deliver it, maybe next week?

As soon as she hung up the phone, Aunt Doris got in her car and drove out Hwy 119 to the Buddy Burger. Momma was back in the office, while two of her girls were cleaning up, getting ready to close at eight. Aunt Doris walked in and stopped in front of the desk where Momma was sitting, sorting through the day's receipts.

"It's a good thing you're sittin' down, Arlene," Aunt Doris said as she walked in, looking straight at Momma very seriously.

"Oh, shit," Momma said, standing up. "What's he done now?" She was absolutely certain that Wesley was either in the emergency room somewhere or in the Grantville police station.

Aunt Doris shook her head.

"No...no, it's not Wesley," she said. "Everybody's fine."

Momma flopped back down in the desk chair and glared with relief at her sister-in-law. "Then good God, Doris...would you mind tellin' me what the devil you drove all the way out here for? Was it just to see if you could make me pee in my pants or what?"

Aunt Doris didn't waste any more time. "Arlene, do you know a Mrs. Holderness...lives up in Riverview somewhere?"

Without hesitation, Momma answered her, "No, I sure don't. Should I?"

"Well, honey, just get ready...'cause you're *gonna* know her. I want you to know, Arlene, that Bertie El Hewitt just called me and said this Mrs. Holderness has a nice piano she wants to *give* Grace...Bertie El was wondering if it'd be OK for them to deliver it *next week*," Doris said, still looking very serious.

Momma squinted, looking hard at Aunt Doris.

"This woman wants to *give* Grace a piano?" she asked, incredulously.

"That's what Bertie El said...said this Mrs. Holderness was at that Christmas luncheon back last month and heard Grace play...then she asked Bertie El about her." Doris was now standing with both hands on her hips.

"...and now this woman wants to *give* Grace a piano?" Momma repeated herself.

"Yep. That's exactly what Bertie El said."

"Doris...are you sure you heard this right?" Momma stood up again, sounding doubtful.

Aunt Doris did not like being doubted.

"Arlene, I *know* what I heard. This Mrs. Holderness.... has a Baldwin spinet piano.... that she wants Grace to have...for *nothing*, no cost, no charge...*nothing*."

There was a long silence. Momma, probably dumbfounded, glanced out the back window of the Buddy Burger office and stood dead still.

Finally Aunt Doris spoke.

"Well...what do you think?"

A slow smile crept across Momma's face; then all of a sudden, she threw up her arms, tossed back her head, and let out a loud rebel yell— "YEEEEEEEEEEEEEHAA!" she bellowed as she rushed from behind the desk. Then she threw her arms around Aunt Doris and swung her around.

"I think HELL YEAH! Do you hear me, Doris?! *HELL* YEAH! Tell 'em we'd *love* to have that piano...tell 'em nothing could tickle us more...tell 'em to bring that baby right on over...*tonight* if they want to!" Momma had Aunt Doris by the shoulders, just a huggin' and shakin' her silly. Aunt Doris told me that it was the most excited she'd ever seen my momma.

So my big, ugly pink piano—that had now, after playing on a Steinway, begun to sound like tin cans pinging together to me—was hauled out of Grammie's parlor by a colored man and his two sons, who took it straight to a honky-tonk called the Blue Note, which had recently opened down near the railroad tracks behind the mill. One of the sons told Grammie that they were going to paint it bright blue; she told him to have at it, because they sure "couldn't hurt it any."

The Baldwin spinet had a beautiful cherry finish, curved legs, a brass lyre desk, and a matching bench to hold some of my music. Mrs. Holderness even sent an antique brass piano light with it, which was just right. When the movers went out the front door, the four of us—Momma, Aunt Doris, Grammie, and I—just stood in the living room, staring at this wonder.

It was spotless. There wasn't a scratch on it anywhere; all the notes were clean and perfect, and even the pedals were shiny. We just stood there for I don't know how long; I thought to myself, childishly, that this even beat a circus train by a long shot.

Grammie was the first one to speak, though her eyes were still focused on the piano. "What do y'all think about a buttermilk pound cake?"

A few seconds passed, and Aunt Doris, bewildered, looked at Grammie, wondering if she had lost her mind or something.

"Momma? What are you talkin' about? A buttermilk pound cake...?"

My momma and I also turned to look at Grammie.

"Well, what do you send somebody who gives you a whole, fine piano? A buttermilk pound cake is all I know to do..." Grammie said, with all sincerity.

We looked at each other. There was certainly something to be said for that idea. After all, anybody who had ever had the honor and pleasure of tasting Grammie's buttermilk pound cake would never underestimate its value, and besides, what else could we do?

Aunt Doris spoke, looking back again at the Baldwin.

"Yeah, come to think of it...that's a good idea, Momma, but Grace"—she turned toward me—"you're gonna have to write Mrs. Holderness a nice note and take it to her with the cake."

Momma looked at me; she was wearing her Buddy Burger uniform and, as usual, reeked of Lucky Strikes. She patted me on the shoulder as she turned to leave. "Yep...that's the least you can do, Gracie. I'll try to find some nice paper for you to use," she said, leaving to get back to work.

"But I don't even know where she lives," I said, picturing myself walking up the hill to Riverview Heights, carrying a pound cake wrapped in heavy aluminum foil and trying to find some big house of a rich lady I didn't even know.

"Don't worry...Bertie El will know," Aunt Doris said confidently.

A few minutes later, I sat down at the spinet and played a few scales and chords. Then I turned on the piano lamp and looked over my shoulder; I was alone. From my stack of Mozart, I found "Turkish March," one of my favorites. I played it all the way through.

When I finished, I just sat there and looked at my new piano, realizing how very lucky I was. I rubbed the top and the edges of the fine wood; I looked again at the beautiful, carved legs, and I opened and closed the cover several times. It was fabulous.

As I sat there drinking it all in, I decided that I would gladly go find this Mrs. Holderness and deliver one mighty-fine pound cake to her, with the nicest note I could manage to write.

I just didn't know how I was going to keep from doing cartwheels and back handsprings all the way up and down Fairview Avenue.

7

Years later, people would say that baseball saved Wesley Stevens. But that spring when Momma let him sign up for Little League, it was just another attempt to head off trouble. His grades had not gotten any worse, but let's just say that he wasn't in any danger of ever being a scholar.

Wesley's PE teacher at school had a brother-in-law, Willis, who was putting together a baseball team of mill-village boys, and the teacher had seen Wesley play pickup games out on the playground. He told Momma that Wesley had a natural swing, had that rhythm and balance that couldn't really be taught; he said it would be a shame for Wesley not to develop it.

Momma told the teacher and his brother-in-law that they were just as welcome as they could be to talk to Wesley and try to get him interested because, the Good Lord knew, nothing she had tried helped. Daddy had been gone nearly a year, and Wesley still had no interest in anything. He mostly slept or sat dazed in front of the television, watching cartoons, when he wasn't in school.

We never knew what this Coach Willis said to Wesley, and Momma said she didn't care, because whatever it was, it worked. Momma gladly paid the $4.50 sign-up fee; then she took Wesley to Rally's and bought him new sneakers, a glove, socks, and a jockstrap.

By mid-April if anyone wanted to see my brother, they had to go to the mill's ball field. Grammie said he ran in the back door every afternoon just long enough to change his clothes, drink a glass of milk, and eat whatever she had put out for him—then he was gone again.

Who knows what caused what; did baseball cause the changes in Wesley, or were the changes already in motion and baseball just magnified them? Either way, Wesley started growing and developing and outgrew three pairs of sneakers in three months.

My brother got taller; he grew muscles, and his feet took on an odor that Momma said she couldn't believe was even human. Nothing but hot water and ammonia could put a dent in the stink of Wesley's shoes and socks. Even Grammie said it beat anything she had ever seen...or smelled.

Wesley Stevens became a Little League star that spring. He played catcher, and he was a home-run hero, and he passed sixth grade with no problem. Grammie and Aunt Doris never missed a game, but Momma worked, and I...well, I had three big fish on my mind by then, so I never saw Wesley play that spring.

Back in early February, Mrs. Hewitt had sat me down one Sunday evening; we were alone, because Hughie was out of town for a family funeral. Mrs. Hewitt had some information she wanted to show me. That was the first I heard of this big state piano competition in Knoxville.

"Grace, I know you can do it. We have to select three classical pieces, none longer than seven minutes; at the competition, the judges will pick which one of the three they want you to perform. It's absolutely essential that you be able to do any one of the three to near perfection... this means you must focus all your time and energy on preparing for the competition," she said.

I listened carefully and wondered if this was something I could actually do. There had to be money involved.

"You really cannot imagine the opportunities that will open up for you by making it to the finals," she said.

Mrs. Hewitt never once asked me directly if I wanted to compete. Somehow I knew she wouldn't have taken no for an answer anyway.

I left her house that night with little confidence about this competition thing. I didn't mention anything she had said to anybody. Then, the following Thursday, she put Chopin's Mazurka in B Minor in front of me, and I was hooked. The work began.

Knoxville—it was only seventy miles away, but it might as well have been on the moon. Without a word to anybody, Mrs. Hewitt paid my entry fee of twenty dollars and began her mission to get me to Knoxville.

A month after the Baldwin spinet was delivered to Grammie's house, the phone rang one night. When Aunt Doris again recognized Bertie El's voice, she thought for sure that something had gone terribly wrong and the Baldwin would have to be returned.

But that was not the case at all. Mrs. Hewitt asked my aunt Doris to come by for tea on Saturday afternoon; she had something important to discuss.

No one could ever have imagined that during that Saturday afternoon, Bertie El Hewitt and Doris Stevens would begin an amazing friendship. For two women from such completely different backgrounds to end-up with so much appreciation for each other was unusual, and it shocked plenty of folks, including me.

While I was at the movies that Saturday night, Momma, Aunt Doris, and Grammie sat down again at the kitchen table, but this time there was no canning jar full of change to count. From what Mrs. Hewitt had told Aunt Doris, as she'd poured tea from her silver teapot earlier that afternoon, it was going to take more than a jar of change to get me to Knoxville.

"She said every contestant must be accompanied by a parent or guardian...and that we should plan on three nights in the Ramada Inn next to the university campus," Aunt Doris explained. "It starts on a Thursday, and the finals are on Saturday afternoon, followed by a banquet that night."

Momma lit another Lucky Strike and looked at Aunt Doris as if she was speaking Chinese.

"Three nights in a hotel...in Knoxville?" Momma said, shaking her head. "Doris, that's a hundred bucks right there if it's a dime."

Aunt Doris just went right on, not missing a beat.

"...and Grace will definitely have to have a new dress, and this time it *has* to be black, Bertie El said."

Maybe if Aunt Doris had told Grammie and Momma *everything* Mrs. Hewitt said, they would have been as determined as she was right from the jump. But what Aunt Doris *didn't* tell them, and didn't tell me, was that this piano competition basically amounted to an audition—a huge audition for several college music scholarships to three different Tennessee schools. *That* fact Aunt Doris kept to herself; she knew to court that kind of hope was out of the question at that point. Just getting to Knoxville was challenge enough for the time being.

Momma pushed back from the kitchen table.

"Well, I would dearly love to see Grace go to this thing, but I don't see how that's gonna happen. I sure can't take three days off from work... and I think we're probably talkin' about at least a hundred and fifty to two hundred dollars by the time it's all said and done," she said as she stood up.

Aunt Doris took a deep breath and looked at Grammie, who didn't have any idea what to say or do.

"Arlene...sit down," my aunt said evenly, looking then directly into Momma's eyes. It did not sound like a friendly invitation, but Momma, a little taken aback, did it anyway. My aunt bit into her lower lip and paused.

"There's a lot riding on this..." Aunt Doris began. "It could change everything for Grace...and I mean *everything*. If we let this slip by... if we can't scratch together a hundred or so dollars to give Grace this chance, then..." She paused and looked around Grammie's cramped, little kitchen and then back into her sister-in-law's eyes. "...then it's all been for nothing—the music lessons, the piano—all of it's been for *nothing*."

Aunt Doris wanted to make my momma see that this was probably the best chance I'd ever have. She took a deep breath.

"Arlene, I know she's *your* daughter, not mine, but..." Aunt Doris stopped. She couldn't find the words without running the risk of really hurting my momma. She tried to think of how to put it, but she couldn't. Finally Aunt Doris, speaking softly, stared straight at Momma and put it very simply.

"We just have to do it...that's all there is to it, Arlene. We *have* to do it."

Momma and Aunt Doris's eyes locked. Maybe it was then that Momma got it; she turned her head and looked away. The sad shadow that often passed across Momma's face, settling in her eyes, surfaced briefly. Momma knew the truth when she heard it.

There was dead quiet; then Grammie broke the silence.

"Well... I can go back to bakin' corn muffins for the Greek's diner. He mentioned it to me again last week, and maybe Grace could work in the afternoons again at the Kress store," Grammie offered.

Aunt Doris shook her head immediately.

"Absolutely not...Grace *cannot* work. All her time, for the next five months, has got to be on the three pieces for the competition. Bertie El says it will be like a full-time job." Aunt Doris paused, "But selling the corn muffins could certainly help a little...and Arlene"—she looked again at my momma—"Bertie El also said we don't have to pay for Grace's lessons. From now on they'll be 'gratis'---that means for free... so right there is some of the money we'll need."

An hour later, the plan was set. Aunt Doris would take off work from the mill office to take me to Knoxville in June. She would make my black dress out of a nice piece of linen she already had. Momma would ask the owner of the Buddy Burger, old Mr. Stancil, if she could have a raise, given that she was already working without one part-time slot filled. And Grammie would clear $1.25 off every dozen corn muffins she sold to Mr. Thakakis at the diner.

When I walked in the back door at Grammie's that night at ten thirty, the three Stevens women told me that I was going to Knoxville.

"You're *goin'*---even if it harelips the governor," Grammie said with determination, re-pinning her bun.

"So I hope you enjoyed the movie tonight, because that's the last one you'll be seeing for a while," Momma said, smiling at Aunt Doris.

Years later, Aunt Doris told me how she lay awake that night, so wired up she couldn't sleep. She said she was so full of frustration and so rankled she could have spit nickels; life was so unfair.

There was Bertie El, wandering around that big, fine house, all alone, with five bedrooms and who-knows-how-many bathrooms, with oriental carpets here and silver tea sets there and so many oil paintings and crystal lamps no one could count 'em all. Aunt Doris said she knew, just as well as she knew her own name, that Bertie El Hewitt could have written a check—right then and there—to cover every bit of my trip to Knoxville and never so much as missed a dime of it.

It wasn't until much later that Aunt Doris figured that maybe, in her own way, Mrs. Hewitt was testing our family. She wanted to see if it meant enough to us, to *me*, to do whatever was necessary to get me to Knoxville so that, just maybe, my talent could get me a chance at a better life.

Aunt Doris said all the scrimpin' and savin' and scratchin' that we would have to do for Knoxville reminded her bitterly of exactly what it had taken, years ago, for Grammie to come-up with the money to pay for Aunt Doris's secretarial course. Grandpa Billy had raised hell about it, but Grammie wouldn't give up.

"If your grandmother had given up, Grace, I would never have gotten my office job at the mill...and I'd probably be moppin' floors or waitin' tables somewhere."

Like Momma, I thought.

Whenever I felt like I couldn't practice another minute, I thought about that and of everything that was being done to help me.

But the person Aunt Doris said she was the most angry at was my daddy—her brother, Hoyt. She said it burned her to the bone that he had up and left not only his own two kids but his own aging momma as well, leaving her—Aunt Doris—to handle whatever came. Nobody, she said, even knew how to reach him or where he was or whether he was dead or alive.

Aunt Doris wondered how it was that some men could walk away and leave their own flesh and blood to root hog or die, all on their own.

"Of all the low-down, rotten things your granddaddy ever did, Grace, at least he *never* did that," she said.

I didn't have any idea what to say back to that.

⌒↺

Mozart's "Turkish March," Chopin's Mazurka in B Minor, and Mendelssohn's Sonata in E, op. 6 took over my life.

I got special permission at school to use my study-hall time to practice on the old baby grand in the auditorium. The girls' advisor allowed me to drop the second semester of chemistry and put me in girls' chorus, where I was allowed to go to the band room and use the upright in there. My grades in math and history dropped, but I still managed to keep a B-minus/C-plus average overall. All the teachers knew what I was preparing for, and that helped.

For hours, while Grammie and Aunt Doris watched Wesley at the baseball field and Momma worked overtime managing the Buddy Burger, I was at the piano. My Sunday evenings with Mrs. Hewitt turned into another weekly lesson in the studio, a lesson that sometimes went for two hours before I got a break.

I only crashed one time.

In early May—it was a Monday—I went to school, and by lunchtime things were nose-diving. I flunked a math quiz; I had horrible menstrual cramps; I lost my favorite lipstick; I forgot my gym suit, and by two o'clock, it was pouring rain. I caught a ride home with Gordy Holloway, and instead of going to Grammie's to practice, I went straight to the garage apartment.

It was quiet, except for the rain pounding the roof, and I was alone. I was drinking some sweet tea, trying to cheer-up and find the energy to get on over to Grammie's to practice, when I made the mistake of looking at myself in the mirror. On my chin was a red zit the size of a jelly bean. It was the last straw—I burst into tears. I lay down on my bed, sobbing. Then I fell sound asleep.

With the rain still falling in sheets, Grammie sent Wesley to find me; when he returned and told her where I was, she said, "Leave her be, Wes," as she took another batch of corn muffins out of the oven.

At nine thirty that night, Momma came in and nudged me.

"Get up, Grace...go brush your teeth and put on your pj's" she said. A few minutes later, she pulled down my bedcovers, and I crawled back in bed.

It rained all night, I think, and no one woke me the next morning. I slept until nearly one o'clock Tuesday afternoon, got up long enough to fix myself a grilled cheese sandwich, and went right back to sleep.

It was the first time I had ever been allowed to miss school for, really, no good reason, and it was the longest I had gone without touching a piano in five years. I was beat.

On Wednesday, the sun was out again, and I felt like my whole head had been cleared and refreshed. Even math class wasn't so bad. I tackled Chopin that afternoon and made big progress, and the giant zit... well, it slowly faded, with the help of makeup and Clearasil. Things were back on track.

School ended just before Memorial Day. I managed to somehow hold on to a straight B average, and Wesley, thank goodness, did not have to go to summer school. That, of course, would have interfered with baseball, and that fact must have kept him motivated enough that he passed all his subjects.

Mrs. Hewitt had a small recital for her students on the last Sunday in May, but I was not included. For the next two weeks, the two weeks before Knoxville, she had me at her house every day, and she and Aunt Doris spoke on the telephone at least once a day, if not twice. Everything, every detail, was discussed; the length of my black dress, the shade of my panty hose, my makeup, my shoes, and my hair. Mrs. Hewitt insisted to Aunt Doris that the black linen dress be completely lined, to avoid my having to wear a slip.

"She's right, Grace...the last thing we'd need is your slip showin'. How tacky would that be?" Aunt Doris said.

I kept wondering when I was going to get nervous, but I must have decided that I didn't need to be; everybody else seemed to be nervous enough for me.

Aunt Doris had Wesley clean up her car; he vacuumed it out, scrubbed the floor mats, washed it, and used Windex on the windows. She said it was the cleanest it had been since she drove it off the lot seven years ago, but it was all for nothing.

On Wednesday evening, Mrs. Hewitt called Aunt Doris.

"Doris, I'm sending Cooper down in the morning at nine for you and Grace. There's plenty of room in my Buick for all of us...and we'll hang the dress, so it won't be crushed," she said.

Aunt Doris hung up the phone and looked at me.

"Who's Cooper?" she asked.

I explained that Cooper was Mrs. Hewitt's colored man, who worked around the house, took care of the car, and did anything else that needed doing that Evelyn didn't do.

"Well, evidently Cooper is drivin' us all to Knoxville," Aunt Doris said, looking at Momma. Grammie said then there was no sense in her packing our lunches, because it wouldn't do for us to be eating fried-egg sandwiches in Bertie El's big Buick.

That night Grammie fixed my favorite dinner—pork chops and coleslaw. Dedee came to do my nails. Momma packed my suitcase with my new black shoes and my new black bra, which Grammie said was just about more than she could stand. According to her, black undergarments were for streetwalkers and strippers, not for young ladies, but Aunt Doris told her again how a white bra strap could easily cause a distraction.

I washed my hair and rolled it on my big brush rollers and went to bed a little early. Oddly, I dreamed about Daddy...something about his wanting to see Wesley's ball game and not being able to find the ballpark.

Momma left for work before I woke up that Thursday morning. She never said anything...not good-bye or good luck or behave yourself or do your best—nothing. All she did was leave a five-dollar bill on the kitchen table and a note scribbled on a paper napkin:

> *Grace, put this in your wallet in case you need anything...*
> *Doris has the cash for everything else—Mom.*

As it turned out, Cooper did not drive us to Knoxville.

Mrs. Hewitt drove, with Aunt Doris sitting in the front seat and me in the back, with my black linen dress hanging in a plastic bag.

Those two talked the *whole* way. It's a good thing I didn't have anything to say, because I might have had to take a breath of oxygen, causing one of them to break their rhythm or miss a beat. I was pretty sure the inside of that Buick had never heard so much nonstop hen chatter. They talked as if they had known each other for thirty years. They talked about clothes and tablecloths and recipes and begonias and Jackie Kennedy and needlepoint and silver polish and Elizabeth Taylor and the last episode of *Dr. Kildare*.

I looked out the window for a while. Then I pulled out my music and glanced again over the notes and arrows Mrs. Hewitt had made on each piece. We stopped once for something to drink, and soon after that, we were on the new section of Interstate 40, going right through Knoxville. As I watched the exits and entrance ramps and all the lanes, I decided it was a good thing that Aunt Doris hadn't driven; no tellin' where we would have ended-up.

Mrs. Hewitt followed the signs for the University of Tennessee and drove us right straight to the building where she said the Music Department was housed. She parked the car, and we got out.

I stopped and looked around; it was the first college campus I had ever seen, and it never crossed my mind that I'd ever see another one.

8

Yes, I was seventeen years old but it was a very young, unsophisticated seventeen.

It had never occurred to me that most of the contestants who had made it to Knoxville had come from cities and densely populated suburbs where they had already faced numerous rounds of fierce competitions and cuts.

All I knew was that before me no one from our rural, backwoods county had ever even *heard* of this event. So you can see, I was a rookie, a punk beginner who didn't even understand that talking and being friendly were out of place, and that this was a serious, playing-for-keeps contest. Buffoon that I was, I was still thinking that, like me, all these kids just loved playing the piano. But by the end of that first day I knew different..

I heard that first day that Myra Meyerson had previously won twice in the lower age groups and was expected to finish- up that year by winning the final big category, the whole shebang, the Senior Advanced Group. But then I showed-up and to be honest, I ended-up really feeling sorry for that girl.

The Senior Advanced Group included fifteen- to eighteen-year-olds, and the competition began on Thursday evening, with thirty-one of us. When the Friday evening competition started, the group was down to seventeen. Then the finals were held on Saturday afternoon, from three to six, in front of a packed auditorium. By then there were only five of us left--three girls and two boys.

In the finals, no one was allowed to play what they had already played for one of the first two cuts, so for me that meant I probably wouldn't play "Turkish March."

Mrs. Hewitt strongly recommended that I play my Chopin Mazurka.

"It's your choice, Grace, but I really think the Chopin is a better bet...the judges haven't heard much Chopin since Thursday," Mrs. Hewitt explained.

I looked at Aunt Doris, who had-- thank the good Lord-- brought her needlepoint with her; otherwise, I think she might have chewed off one of her own arms or something—she was that nervous. As it was, she was stabbing at the floral canvas of a pillow cover as if she was putting out her boss's left eye or something. She didn't even look up as she spoke.

"Grace, listen to Bertie El...and do what she says," Aunt Doris ordered. "She knows what she's talkin' about."

So I played the Chopin, and for luck, Mrs. Hewitt had me wear a strand of her pearls; it was eighteen inches long.

"I thought about bringing my matinee-length strand," she said, fastening the gold clasp, "but that would have been far too much...this princess length is just right for you," she said.

Aunt Doris gasped when I turned around; the pearls were the perfect touch against the black linen. I reached up to touch them, but Aunt Doris gently slapped my hand away. "Don't touch 'em," she whispered so Mrs. Hewitt couldn't hear. "They probably cost more than my car."

As I walked out on the stage for the finals, I still had no idea what winning this whole shootin' match might mean. The size of the crowd didn't bother me, since I'd already played for over a hundred people back at the Country Club luncheon. And the beautiful concert-grand Steinway didn't intimidate me.

I guess the only things that made me a little nervous were the lights; the auditorium was completely dark, and the lights beamed down, creating a glowing circle around the piano. There was no way to see anybody's face or to have any idea of how full the place really was, which was probably just as well.

The five finalists drew numbers to determine the order of our performances; I got third, which I figured was pretty lucky—right smack in the middle, not too early, not too late. No one could be backstage with us as we waited in a nice sitting room. I tried talking to one of the other girls, but she wasn't too friendly, and neither of the boys said a word. They had all been in this competition before.

I guess you could say that if I'd had enough sense to know what was at stake, I would have been shaky and nervous, or at least a little scared, but I wasn't. And to tell you the truth, it all happened fast.

They called for "Finalist number three", I walked-out, sat down, took a deep breath and let it go. Once I started playing, everything else faded away and it was just me and Chopin and that wonderful instrument. Nothing showed-- no bra straps or hem threads-- and there were no stumbles or fumbles or memory lapses. There was just a young woman in a black dress wearing pearls on a stage playing a grand piano....and at that moment in time it just happened to be me.

The next thing I knew there was applause and I was bowing. Then I smiled as I walked off the stage because somehow I just knew that, no matter what, that moment would be one of my all-time favorite memories, pearls and all.

Forty minutes after the last contestant played, we five were standing on the stage as the final results were announced. The spotlights were on us, but some of the other house lights were on by then, so we weren't totally blinded.

Third place went to the boy from Lone Oak; he took his trophy and his certificate and walked off the stage.

Then they called Myra Meyerson's name.

Now let me explain: Myra's mother, a pediatrician in Chattanooga, and her father, a high-school music teacher, were both there. Aunt Doris said the doctor- mother came close to having a conniption fit out in the lobby afterwards as one of the officials gently led Dr. Meyerson away but not before she complained nastily about that "little hick nobody," meaning me, I guess. Clearly this Grantville constituency from East Tennessee had blindsided some folks.

So there on the stage they called Myra's name, and you could hear a genuine gasp just as the applause began. Myra started crying as she walked forward, probably knowing that her momma would take that second-place finish much worse than Myra took it. She tried to smile as she left the stage, but she just couldn't, bless her heart. I thought to myself that this whole thing must mean the very world to her if she was willing to cry in front of all these people.

Aunt Doris said later that the poor young'un was probably crying because she had to face her momma.

Left then on stage were the three of us; I was standing in the middle, with the boy from Jackson on my left and the short girl from Memphis on my right.

At that point, I figured I had done what Mrs. Hewitt wanted—I had made it to the finals, and that was more than anybody from Grantville had ever done for sure. I was pretty satisfied; it had been quite an experience—getting to go to Knoxville, staying in the Ramada Inn for three nights, seeing the UT campus, and wearing a strand of real pearls—and there was still the banquet that night to look forward to.

"...*Grace Jeanette Stevens!*" the man at the microphone said loudly, the sound blaring through the auditorium speakers just as the applause started.

I didn't move—wondering if I had actually heard it right. Did he say Grace Jeanette Stevens? I thought to myself. The boy from Jackson and the girl from Memphis both started clapping, and a lady carrying a white and bronze statue suddenly walked out on stage and stopped almost right in front of me.

"Honey, you won...walk on up there," she said over the applause, nudging me forward and smiling. I still wasn't sure that I had actually heard my own name, but she seemed pretty sure of it, so I walked up to the man with the microphone.

"...and Grace is from Grantville in East Tennessee, where she studies piano under Mrs. Roberta Hewitt. Is Mrs. Hewitt here?" the man asked, squinting into the lights.

And, of course, Mrs. Hewitt was there; she stepped into the aisle from her seat beside Aunt Doris and waved and bowed slightly to the crowd. She looked straight at me and threw me a kiss, which surprised me to no end; then she turned to throw her arms around Aunt Doris again as the applause died off.

Moments later, I was surrounded by people congratulating me, photographers taking my picture holding the white-and-bronze statue, and some of the younger contestants, who handed me flowers. It was all pretty amazing, and I remember thinking that it was hard to believe all this had come to me from simply doing something I dearly loved to do—play the piano.

9

"CONGRATSULATIONS ON GRACE!"

That's what the banner that Mr. and Mrs. Thakakis painted and hung above the front door of the diner said. Momma and Wesley thought it was hilarious, but everybody understood; the point was Mr. Thakakis gave a pig roast and invited everybody from Mount Vernon Baptist, all my high-school friends, and all the mill-village families who wanted to come. It was on a Sunday afternoon, so Momma got to go, and we all had a blast. Mrs. Hewitt was invited, but she said she just couldn't make it, which Momma said was just as well; somehow the words "Mrs. Hewitt" and "pig roast" didn't connect, I guess.

The rest of the summer flew by. I worked part time again at the Kress store, and I finally got to see Wesley play baseball.

My picture was on the front page of the Grantville newspaper again, and there was an article about the piano competition in Knoxville. It even mentioned the statue I won, which Mrs. Hewitt explained was a Roman goddess of music, a muse, holding a bronze lyre. It was placed on the left end of my piano at Grammie's. Wesley, the comic, said it didn't look anything like me. Grammie threatened to shave his head if he ever so much as touched it.

Mrs. Holderness gave a tea in my honor; Momma couldn't go because of work, and Grammie said she would be too nervous to go, so Aunt Doris went with me. I stood in a receiving line for the first time in my life, right between Mrs. Holderness and Mrs. Hewitt, and shook hands with dozens of people I had never met before.

The black linen dress was sent to the dry cleaners and placed in the back of my closet. Mrs. Hewitt received two copies of a good picture of me taken in Knoxville while I was wearing the pearls. Aunt Doris framed it, and it, too, was placed on my piano.

For the rest of the summer, I simply played and enjoyed my music. I did a little Hanon, but other than that, I just played whatever I wanted whenever I wanted to. I even played a new and improved rendition of "Beulah Land" for Grammie.

Mrs. Hewitt said I deserved a break, and I think she probably did, too. She never mentioned to anyone, not even Aunt Doris, that Vanderbilt University was going to be contacting me, probably sometime in the fall.

It's amazing how one little thing can change so much. Just before school started, I actually became good friends with Susie Ackerman, Leslie Joan Underwood, and Baylin Nelson; they were all cheerleaders. Baylin had a new yellow Camaro, and the four of us would go to Monk's on Friday nights. Jimmy Dale Littlepage, one of the football players, was shy and quiet, but suddenly every time I turned around, he was right at my elbow.

Evidently just playing the piano and winning a contest had become my ticket into this group of cool seniors, the kids who mostly lived in Crestview. As far as I was concerned, that was a huge step above living in the mill village in a garage apartment, but none of them gave any thought to that. I was just really glad that the Buddy Burger was completely on the other side of town so that it was not so obvious that my momma not only worked, she worked at Buddy Burger.

By mid-September Aunt Doris was finished with my new school clothes for fall. Her sewing skills were amazing; if I saw something in a movie or in a magazine that I wanted, all I had to do was sort of sketch it out, and Aunt Doris could make it. She would either find a pattern that was close, or she'd make her own pattern for it. I don't think any of my friends realized that most of my wardrobe was homemade.

There was no telephone at our garage apartment. We used Grammie's telephone number, and, of course, the phone number at the Buddy Burger. All of my paper work in Knoxville only had Grammie's number on it, so it was reasonable that Vanderbilt University used that number to try to reach us in early October.

Aunt Doris said later that it was just sad, bad luck that the only person home that afternoon was Wesley; he answered the phone.

The secretary for the vice-president of Vanderbilt University asked to speak to either of the parents of Grace Stevens. Wesley told her that Momma, Arlene Stevens, could be reached at the Buddy Burger; then he gave her the number.

Now keep in mind, it was a Thursday afternoon, and although the lunch rush at the Buddy Burger was over, a truck had arrived, and Momma was in the middle of inventorying all the cases as they were unloaded into the freezer. And, wouldn't you know it, one of the afternoon girls had called in sick, so it was only Momma and Edna there right then, doing everything.

Momma was really busy, and when the phone started ringing, she let it ring and ring and ring. Finally she couldn't stand it any longer—she dashed into the office and snatched up the receiver.

As with all burger joints and bars, I guess, there's always the occasional prank caller. Momma had endured her share of "Is Bob Wire there?" and "This is the Tennessee National Guard, and we want to order three thousand, seven hundred and fifty-four hamburgers," and other such nonsense. She said it was just kids messin' around.

When the lady in Nashville heard Momma answer the phone and say, "Buddy Burger," she responded simply, saying, "This is the secretary for the vice-president of Vanderbilt University and—"

That was as far as she got.

Momma was covered- up, and she was *not* in the mood for some smartass playing on the telephone.

"Oh really?" she snapped. "Well, this is the White House, and I'm Lady Bird Johnson. I'm busy plantin' shrubs!" she yelled into the phone then slammed it down. At least she didn't tell the caller what she was famous for saying: "Kiss my ass."

That night the five of us sat around the kitchen table. Vanderbilt had called Mrs. Hewitt, and when she called Aunt Doris at work, it was to say that there was no excuse for this, that it was uncalled for and absolutely mortifying, and that Grace's mother must be "a special kind of uncouth." Bertie El was livid.

The kitchen was quiet. Aunt Doris was trying not to say anything more to Momma, who was upset enough; Grammie was nervously fiddling with her hairpins, and Wesley was sullen, having been cross-examined then lectured that this was *not* funny.

I just sat there in a daze, *Vanderbilt University*? Vanderbilt University was trying to reach Momma on my behalf?

THE Vanderbilt University? It just couldn't be true.

"Grace, I'm so sorry," Momma said again. "Honey, I just didn't think it was real...and I was busy, and I was shorthanded...and"—she reached for another Lucky—"and I just screwed up. That's all there is to it."

I couldn't even be mad at Momma; I was still in shock. *Vanderbilt University*? I managed to just nod my head and look at her.

Aunt Doris unfolded her arms and sat forward, putting her hands on the table.

"Well..." she said, "the good news is that Bertie El said they'll be callin' back, probably tomorrow, so this is what we need to do. Arlene, if they call you at work, how about you give them my name and work number...and explain that it might be best if they talk to me? Does that suit you?" she asked, knowing full well that it would.

"Why hell, yes, Doris...it's better for you to talk to 'em," Momma said, flicking her ashes into an old State Bank ashtray.

Then Aunt Doris looked at Grammie.

"And, Momma, if they call here, you ask them to leave a number so that Grace's momma...or her aunt...can call them back. OK?"

"I sure will..." Grammie said, glad to know her part in the plan.

Then we all looked at Wesley.

"It's not my fault!" he said again. "All I did was answer the phone and tell them where Momma was!"

Grammie reached over and patted Wesley's arm.

"It's all right, Wes...you didn't do anything wrong," she assured him.

"But, Wesley," Aunt Doris said, *"If..."* She paused here and emphasized the "if." *"IF*...they call again and you happen to answer the phone, just be very polite and call Grammie to the phone...and if—God help us—no one else happens to be here, just *take down the number*...and, Wes, you've *got* to get it right. Do you understand? You've *got* to get the phone number right. It's very important," she added.

Wesley stood up.

"OK...OK...I'll get it right," he said, turning to leave the kitchen.

"Gram, can I watch *Hawaii Five-O*?"

After we heard the television in the front bedroom come on, Grammie, Momma, and Aunt Doris looked at me. At last the startling, real possibility of it all sank in for me. A slow smile crept over my face as I looked around the table. Our eyes darted around as the four of us glanced at each other, and then—suddenly—we were all grinning, shaking our heads in disbelief, biting our lips to keep from hootin' and hollerin', all of us about to bust wide-open.

Momma was the first to speak.

"Good God Almighty, Gracie...*Vanderbilt University*," she said softly, smiling and staring at me as if she wasn't sure exactly who I was.

Aunt Doris reached over and put her arm around me, giving me a firm shake. "Yep...Vanderbilt," she said, beaming, sounding thrilled to pieces.

"Grace Stevens from Grantville...a Vanderbilt co-ed."

I hardly slept that night.

❧

Roland Stancil—some people called him R. T.—grew up on a farm in East Tennessee with his two brothers. Their dad, Roland Stancil Sr., was killed in 1933 when the Bush Hog he was driving flipped over on him. Evidently that was not uncommon back then.

Anyway, Roland's momma and her three boys then moved in with old Mrs. Stancil, a widow herself, who had opened a little café on the side of a county road that would eventually become Highway 119.

All three Stancil boys went into the Army after Pearl Harbor. The youngest, Arthur—Artie for short—was killed in France, but R. T. and Frank made it back. Frank stayed in the service and made a good career of it. R. T. came home and soon married Dr. Foster's only daughter, Judith.

Another thing R. T. did when he got home was take over his grannie's café, and when she died in 1950, he turned it into the Buddy Burger with carhops and a jukebox. By then Highway 119 had been widened, and the Buddy Burger boomed.

Judith decided that flippin' burgers for the rest of her life while she raised her own two boys was not what she had in mind. She went off to Knoxville and took a dental-assistant course and then went to work for her own daddy, cleanin' teeth and trimmin' gums.

Aunt Doris used to say that she couldn't think of a nastier job than "diggin' and pokin' around in somebody's mouth," but she guessed somebody had to do it. I guess good dental health and hygiene were not exactly a top priority for most people in Grantville, especially the mill families.

Judith and R. T. built one of the first brick ranch houses—a fine three-bedroom, two-bath house, with a double carport—in the new subdivision called Crestview, and both the Stancil boys, twins, did well in school and went on to the University of Tennessee.

That is, they went on to college after their momma up and died suddenly in 1961—a brain hemorrhage they said—leaving R. T. to get his sons the rest of the way through high school then off to Knoxville. It was around that time that he stopped running the Buddy Burger himself and hired a manager.

Roland T. Stancil was a solid citizen and business owner, the secretary of the local VFW, a member of the Kiwanis and Elks, a deacon of Disciple United Methodist Church—and he was lonely.

To me, Mr. Stancil was old...really old. Maybe not as old as Grammie, but he was, for sure, older than Aunt Doris and Momma. It wasn't until later on that I realized that fifty-two is not ancient by any stretch.

Just when it was that he fell in love with my momma—the third, and he said *best* manager he had hired for the Buddy Burger—is still unknown. Mr. Stancil never let on to a single soul that he thought Arlene Stevens was a fine, hardworking, honest woman who was far smarter than her tenth-grade education might indicate. He saved all that for later, but the trouble was, Mr. Stancil assumed that Momma was divorced. She wasn't.

What Momma was assuming about R. T. Stancil, her boss, was evidently very little. He had given Momma a raise every chance he got, and he had also given her more and more responsibility for the Buddy Burger, which was now making more money than ever. He credited Momma with that. She didn't think anything of it when sometimes late on Saturday evenings, around closing time, he would show up and sit around, chatting with her back in the office. It was, after all, *his* business, and he had a right to be there anytime he wanted, she said.

Momma was now making seventy-five dollars a week, and she had hired another full-time lady who could be trusted. That meant Momma was now available to meet with Wesley's teachers and to be more involved at his school. By then I was a senior, and she knew I had both Aunt Doris and Mrs. Hewitt standing over me most of the time. Wesley still needed all the attention and encouragement she could give him.

Momma had also begun to talk about moving us into a duplex not far from the high school, but first she had to pay off the loan on her Corvair.

Jimmy Dale Littlepage came around Grammie's house a lot, especially on Thursdays, when he didn't have football practice and knew I'd be walking up the hill to my music lesson. He sometimes even appeared at the corner when I left Mrs. Hewitt's house, and he'd walk me back home.

If Wesley was around, Jimmy Dale would horse around with him awhile out in the yard. He really wasn't around *that* much, but Aunt Doris made the comment that it looked as if Jimmy Dale wanted us "to take him to raise." Grammie said she thought he was a very nice young man. Jimmy Dale finally got around to asking me to the homecoming dance in early November. He borrowed his family's Impala, and we had a good time.

Jimmy Dale was a really good linebacker, I guess, and by Thanksgiving there were two different small colleges looking at him. He ended up going to Carson Newman.

Aunt Doris drove me to Nashville a week before Thanksgiving to meet with the scholarship committee at Vanderbilt. An 8 mm film, with sound, of the piano competition had been reviewed by two different Vanderbilt boards, so I didn't have to play the piano for them at all, which I had certainly come prepared to do, thanks to Mrs. Hewitt.

After the interview, they arranged for us to have a tour of the campus and to meet with some of the Music Department faculty. They said most of their music-scholarship students earned degrees in music education, with a minor in another subject they wanted to teach. On one floor of the Music Department, there seemed to be room after room of practice studios, private little nooks with nice practice pianos, where students could work on their music.

It was lucky for me that they didn't ask me any questions, because I had no idea what they were talking about. Hours, credits, majors, minors, performance labs, internships—none of that made any sense to me, but they said all their freshmen got their own counselor who could help with all that.

We only stayed one night, but before we left to come home the next afternoon, I had to fill out several forms regarding the scholarship. They gave me lots of other sheets of information to take home with me, one of which said that my ACT score and my high-school grades at graduation would have to be submitted as soon as possible and no later than May 15.

On the trip home that evening, Aunt Doris told me that unless I really messed something up, it looked as if I had a college scholarship to Vanderbilt University to study music. I stared out the car window for a long time, thinking about that. It was all pretty unbelievable. A few minutes later, I asked Aunt Doris for a favor.

"Aunt Doris, would it be all right if we didn't tell anybody else about this right now?"

She glanced over at me and then back at the road, not saying anything.

"I mean... of course Grammie and Momma know...and Mrs. Hewitt... but I really don't want it broadcast all over town...at least not now," I explained, looking over at her.

I could just see another picture of myself in the newspaper, announcing my scholarship to Vanderbilt University. I wasn't ready for that. Winning a contest in Knoxville was one thing, going to Vanderbilt University was altogether another.

Aunt Doris still didn't say anything. It was dark, and we had run into a steady rain as we'd driven east. After a few miles, the traffic thinned out, and she spoke.

"Grace, we don't have to say a word to anybody, if that's what you want...but, honey, what's wrong? Aren't you happy about this? Don't you understand what an accomplishment this is?"

I turned to stare out the window again. I wasn't sure what I really felt about it all, and I sure didn't know what to say to Aunt Doris.

I guess the truth was I was scared. If everything worked out, I'd graduate from high school in May, and then I'd leave Grantville. I'd move to Nashville and go live at college with a bunch of other people I didn't know, leaving behind everything and everybody I'd ever known. And yeah, it wasn't really *that* far to Nashville, but Nashville wasn't home. In fact nowhere else was home but where Momma and Wesley and Grammie were. As always at big moments, I could still hear Daddy's words: *who did I think I was anyway?*

Aunt Doris basically read my mind—there's no other explanation for what she said to me next.

"Grace...I want you to remember something. You have a true, natural talent for the piano. God knows, I don't know where it came from.... but I do know that you have it, and maybe the reason you have it is because it's meant to be your ticket out of living paycheck to paycheck, out of scrimpin' and scratchin' and never gettin' ahead. Grantville will *always* be there, honey...it's not goin' anywhere... and most of the people there aren't goin' anywhere, but if you get a chance to leave and get an education...to go *use* your talent...no one who really cares about you would want you to miss out on that. You can *always* come back home—you can always decide later on that Grantville is where you want to be...you can make a choice then to come back—come back on *your* terms, not because you don't have anything else. You know I'll help you all I can. I'll make your clothes, and I'll drive over to see you, and I'll try to help you with some spendin' money, but, Grace, you can't turn this down...you can't let yourself think that there's *anything* in Grantville, Tennessee, worth givin' up this chance. Ten years from now, you'd be sick—absolutely sick, I'm tellin' you—to think what you gave up. You'd be kickin' yourself for the rest of your life."

I listened to everything Aunt Doris said, and somewhere deep inside me, I knew she was right. But I knew, too, that to leave the mill village and go fit-in on a college campus was going to be a huge, painful leap into the unknown for me. How in the name of bejesus am I gonna pull that off? I wondered.

The only thing that I felt confident about at that moment was my music. As long as I had that, as long as my Chopin and Beethoven and Liszt and Schubert were going with me, I figured I could probably do it—somehow.

A few minutes later, I looked at my aunt.

"I'm gonna do it, Aunt Doris. I just need some time to think about it. I'd rather wait until the spring...maybe closer to graduation...before I tell everybody," I said.

Aunt Doris smiled.

"That's fine with me, Grace, but we'll probably have to sit on Bertie El to keep her quiet."

Nobody locked their cars in Grantville. They just didn't do it. Maybe it was because most people just stayed on their side of town, where everybody knew whose car was whose and who ought to be in it and who shouldn't— I don't know. But three days before Christmas, on her way home from work, Momma stopped by Miller's and locked her keys in the car.

Wesley brought the spare key from the kitchen drawer in the apartment over to Aunt Doris, so she could drive down to Miller's Discount Bin, where Momma was waiting in the parking lot.

Aunt Doris pulled up beside Momma and rolled down the window.

"Here you go, Arlene." She handed the key to her. The weather had turned cold, and Aunt Doris noticed that Momma's eyes and nose were red from standing out in the wind, but something else didn't seem right. Aunt Doris parked her car and got out.

"Thanks for comin', Doris. I hate that you had to drive all the way out here," Momma said, not lookin' up at all.

"I don't mind, Arlene... but since when do you lock your car? Do you really think anybody wants this crazy, little blue box you're drivin' around in?" Aunt Doris kidded, hoping to get a smile from Momma.

There was no smile. Momma unlocked her door and then looked at her sister-in-law.

"Go around and get in, Doris. I wanna show you somethin'."

Without a word, my aunt, feeling concerned now, got in the passenger seat and closed the door. Momma started the engine to warm up the car and then just sat there.

"What is it, Arlene? Are you OK?"

Momma looked at Aunt Doris hard, and then finally she reached over and opened the glove compartment. She reached in and got a small, black velvet box out and handed it to Aunt Doris. Without a word, my aunt opened the box—and gasped. Inside was a beautiful diamond ring.

"Where did you *get* this?" Aunt Doris was looking at the ring, absolutely mesmerized. It was a nice, bright chunk of rock on a gold band.

Momma didn't answer.

Aunt Doris sat there, holding this gorgeous ring, her mouth still hanging open. She tried again.

"Arlene? Where did you get this? Whose is it?"

Momma had turned away and was looking out the driver-side window. She wasn't crying, but she was upset, Aunt Doris told me later.

"Arlene?" Aunt Doris was looking at Momma now.

Finally Momma turned toward Aunt Doris and spoke.

"It's mine. R. T. Stancil asked me to marry him."

Aunt Doris laughed later on, when she realized that the first thing she thought was, *this is why she locked the car!*

By ten o'clock that night, when neither Momma nor Aunt Doris were home, Grammie and me—I mean Grammie and I—began to get worried. Then the phone rang. I beat Grammie to it.

"Grace, we're fine...tell your Grammie we'll be home in about an hour," Aunt Doris said.

She didn't give me a chance to ask where they were or what they were doing. I found out later that they drove over to an all-night truck stop out by the interstate; they got coffee and talked. Grammie didn't believe them, but she didn't say anything.

Momma told Aunt Doris how R. T. had come by last week and suggested that she close the Buddy Burger a little early the week of Christmas, which she had done. Her girls were glad to get the time off to finish up their Christmas shopping and baking and what have you.

So tonight, when Edna left and Momma went to lock up, there in the back door of the Buddy Burger stood Mr. Stancil. He was dressed up, said he was headed over to a Kiwanis Christmas party and just thought he'd stop by. They went into the office, and before Momma could even sit down at the desk, Mr. Stancil reached out suddenly and tapped her arm.

She told Aunt Doris that at first it sort of scared her, because he had never so much as touched her before then. But you know Momma, even being a little startled doesn't stop her; apparently she whirled around right fast and was ready for anything when Mr. Stancil just reached right out, and handed her the little velvet box.

"Arlene, I want you to marry me." That's all he said.

Momma told Aunt Doris that she damned near staggered backward and that he had to reach out to steady her, until finally she just leaned her backside up against the desk, her hands shaking as she opened the box.

Aunt Doris, of course, wanted to know what Momma had said, and Momma, still stunned I guess, couldn't remember saying a word. She said she thinks she just stood there, or rather just leaned there, "lookin' at him like a cow starin' at a new gate."

"You don't have to answer me right now," Mr. Stancil said, "but I want you to think about it. I know this is a bit of a shock, but I've come to see what a fine woman you are, and I think we can have a good life together."

I'm sure Mr. Stancil stood there a minute or two, thinking surely Momma would say *something*, but she never did. He went on to tell her that he was fifty-two years old, in good health, financially sound, and a Methodist. When she still didn't speak, he finally just said he'd better get on over to the party and he hoped maybe they could see each other sometime tomorrow.

Momma said she didn't really remember locking up the Buddy Burger, and she didn't remember driving to Miller's. She said the next thing she knew, she was walking across the parking lot when it suddenly hit her that she had locked the car because of the velvet box—and the keys were still in the ignition.

Needless to say, the diamond ring was put back in the glove compartment of Momma's car, and this time she locked the glove box, which, of course, had also never been done before.

She swore Aunt Doris to secrecy. No, that's not true. What she actually did was threaten to snatch Aunt Doris bald-headed and slit her tires if she told anybody—*anybody*, "any living soul about this"—and that included Grammie and Bertie El and Dedee and every other two-legged creature on the planet.

Aunt Doris, of course, agreed to not say a word to anybody, but she just *had* to ask the biggest question of all.

"Arlene, what are you gonna do?"

What Momma did was go to work early the next morning and call Mr. Stancil. She asked him to come to the Buddy Burger as soon as he could, which he did. Once Edna got there, Momma and Mr. Stancil went into the office and closed the door, which evidently they had never done.

Momma told him right up front that she couldn't marry him—in fact, she couldn't marry anybody, because she was still married to Hoyt Stevens and had no idea where he was or how to reach him, making a divorce pretty much impossible. From the pocket of her Buddy Burger uniform, Momma pulled out the velvet box to hand to Mr. Stancil, but he didn't take it. She put it on the edge of the desk.

What Mr. Stancil did then was sit down in the desk chair and ask Momma—just as straight and direct as anything—if she *wanted* a divorce.

No one had ever asked her that question, so when R. T. sat down and put that question out there, Momma sat down, too, on a stack of big boxes of ketchup and mustard jars, still sitting by the door because she hadn't unloaded them the night before, and actually thought about it.

A few minutes later, she looked at him and spoke.

"Come to think of it, I *do* want a divorce. He's been gone for over two years...he's never sent me a dime to help with the kids...he hasn't even seen or talked to his own momma or sister all that time...and the more I think about it, I'm better off now than I was when he was around...and I think my kids are too."

That was all R. T. had to hear.

He told Momma to put that velvet box somewhere safe for the time being. Then he asked her if she'd be OK with his attorney looking into finding Hoyt Stevens in order to initiate divorce proceedings.

"That's fine with me, but I don't have the money to pay for a divorce...and there's no tellin' what it will take to find that jackass." Momma looked away, feeling a little embarrassed at her language. "He said he was going down to Mobile, but we don't even have an address or anything," she added.

Mr. Stancil said that the money part of it was not going to be a problem and that however long it took, well, it'd just have to take—but it could, and would, be done.

Then he asked Momma to the New Year's Eve dance at the Elks Lodge.

On the third Tuesday in January, it started snowing. All the schools closed at noon, and by the time it was over, East Tennessee had over a foot of snow on the ground—the biggest snowfall most of us could remember. Everything was canceled or postponed, including Mrs. Hewitt's lessons.

For two days we all played outside—there was slipping and sliding on everything from water skis to cookie sheets; there were snowmen and snowball fights and snow huts. It was great fun for everybody, even some of the grown-ups, since almost everything was closed.

On Thursday evening, Mrs. Hewitt called and asked if I'd like to come by. Her help had not been able to get there, and I guess she had a little cabin fever, so I bundled up and walked up the hill. She had also called Hughie to see if he wanted to come, but he was busy, cleaning one of his fish tanks.

Mrs. Hewitt and I listened to her new Van Cliburn album while we had hot chocolate and popcorn, which she said she hadn't tasted in years. We talked about our favorite composers and our favorite pieces of music; then, out of the blue, she asked me about my birthday. I told her that on May 3, three weeks before graduation, I'd have my eighteenth birthday.

I don't know whether she had been planning something all along, or whether it just popped into her head right then and there, but she told me that she would very much like to host something special for me—maybe a combination recital/birthday/graduation party. She said she was sure Aunt Doris would be willing to help and that it would be the perfect opportunity for me to perform for my family and closest friends, as well as for some of her dearest friends and neighbors, before I went away to college.

"Come with me, Grace," Mrs. Hewitt said, suddenly standing up from her chair. I followed her out of the sun-room, through the dining room, to the front of the big house, where, in an alcove, sat her black, glossy piano. We stopped, and she switched on the big chandelier overhead.

"Now just imagine...we can move the piano forward just a little and have two or three dozen chairs placed here." She motioned toward the area near the stairs. "Then we can have a nice buffet in the dining room, followed by birthday cake. How does that sound?" she asked, smiling at me.

I couldn't believe what I was hearing—Mrs. Hewitt was going to invite *my* family and friends into *her* house and then let *me* play on her custom-made, one-of-a-kind, magnificent piano? She was still standing there, smiling at me, wanting me to respond, and all I wanted was for someone to pinch the stew out of me, so I'd wake up; this was obviously just a dream. Finally I managed to mumble a semi-coherent answer as I stared at that piano.

"Oh, Mrs. Hewitt...I can't think of anything more wonderful."

Before I left there that evening, she helped me decide what music I would most like to play, and she suggested one new Mozart sonata, no. 13 in B Flat, that she would teach me, along with the second movement of the *Moonlight Sonata*, before May. Mrs. Hewitt said she would have invitations and programs printed up sometime in April, so we had plenty of time.

As I left her house that night, I was still stunned at this whole idea,

Mrs. Hewitt did something else that completely surprised me. As I was pulling on my gloves and buttoning my coat, I said, as usual, "Thank you, Mrs. Hewitt."

She touched my arm gently and said, "Grace, I think it's time for you to call me something besides Mrs. Hewitt...after all, you're more to me than just one of my students and..."

She didn't finish; she just stood there, smiling at me. I looked at her and had no idea what to say.

"From now on, how about you call me Bertie El?" she suggested.

My eyes immediately widened, and she quickly saw that I couldn't do that; there was no way that would do.

"Oh, I see.....well then... how about just Miss Bertie? How's that?" she asked, smiling.

Then I smiled, too. She had a point; she and I had spent a lot of time together, and she had taught me more than just music lessons, and she had become good friends with Aunt Doris.

"Yes, ma'am...Miss Bertie," I said, then I turned and went out the door. She waited at the door and left the driveway lights on until I was down the street and turning to go down the hill.

There was no traffic, and everything was still and quiet. The snow in the yards of the big houses in Riverview was untouched and perfect; the air was cold and clear, and I could see my breath. The streetlights seemed brighter than usual; there were none of the usual sounds—no buses in the distance, no barking dogs or whistles from the mill. Almost everything was closed up and silent; that's what happens in the South when that much snow falls. I looked up and saw a huge full moon rising in the eastern sky.

That same moon was shining over Vanderbilt University, and it was shining over Knoxville, and it was shining over my daddy, wherever he was. Someday, I figured...yes, someday maybe he'd know that sometimes it doesn't hurt to think that who you are might be a little bit special after all.

I went to sleep that night thinking about Miss Bertie's grand piano and how I used to look through the window at it on Halloween nights. I could never have imagined what was ahead.

Aunt Doris said there was "nothing, nothing...I'm here to tell you," that, given enough money and enough time, a good lawyer couldn't do.

Apparently R. T. Stancil had the money and was willing to take the time for his lawyer to hire whoever needed to be hired to find my daddy. Off-duty police officers, private investigators, other lawyers in Alabama, Mississippi, and Louisiana, detectives, and insurance specialists—they were all hired on and off in various locations. Billy Hoyt Stevens was going to be found, one way or another.

Momma never said a word to Wesley or me, but one night in March, Aunt Doris sat us both down at Grammie's kitchen table. She said it might not be her place to do it, but she knew that we were old enough to know the truth, and she was going to tell us.

According to my aunt, my momma was still a young, attractive woman, and it only made sense that after nearly three years with no word from Daddy, something needed to be done—legally.

Wesley, who never got another card or anything from Daddy after that first Christmas, must've still held some kind of pitiful hope that Daddy was going to come back home. I knew better; plus look at all the good things that had happened without Daddy being around. I didn't even mind our little garage apartment anymore. The only thing that bothered me was how sad Grammie always looked whenever someone mentioned Hoyt Stevens. No matter what, he was still her son, and I knew she loved him.

"So they're gettin' divorced?" Wesley asked angrily.

"I think so, Wesley...that is, if somebody can manage to find him sometime before we're all dead and gone," Aunt Doris said. "It's for the best, because he evidently doesn't give a happy damn about y'all or me or even your grandmother," she added. "And there's no sense in your momma bein' tied to him any longer."

Wesley didn't say a word; he got up from the table and walked out the back door, letting it slam shut. A few minutes later, we could hear him bouncing a baseball off the back steps and catching it in an old fielder's glove that had been Daddy's. Wesley had passed many hours catching that baseball like that since the season ended last summer.

Grammie walked over and looked out the back window at him.

"He needs a jacket on," she said.

"Just leave him alone, Momma," Aunt Doris replied, turning back toward me.

Aunt Doris told me then that Mr. Stancil had asked Momma to marry him and that she was thinking seriously about taking him up on it, if his lawyers did manage to get her cut loose from Daddy. My aunt asked me what I thought about that.

Maybe something in me had already begun to separate from Momma and Grantville and our little world there in the mill village. I would soon be eighteen years old; in two months I would graduate from high school, and three months after that, I'd be leaving for Vanderbilt. I was headed toward a new life. Why shouldn't Momma have a chance at a new—maybe easier—life?

"Mr. Stancil's OK, I guess, but he's kinda old, isn't he?" I said, looking at Aunt Doris and Grammie.

"He's thirteen years older than your momma...he's a good Christian man who's financially comfortable," my aunt said. "And he thinks the world of her."

Those last words really hit me.

There was a movie I could play in my head anytime I wanted to. In it I was a little kid again, back in our mill-village house, and I could see and hear, plain as day, all the times my daddy yelled and cussed at Momma; all the times he criticized her and called her stupid, blaming her for things I knew weren't her fault; all the times he never did anything on her birthday or on Mother's Day or even at Christmas; all the times he never came home on payday, staying all night at the Cozy Corner; and then how he raised hell when Momma went to work. And one of the saddest, most vivid gashes in my memory was the image of that shelf on the kitchen floor, surrounded by all her little blue dishes, that he had jerked off the wall and smashed. The movie ended abruptly right there, returning to the cold storage of my childhood.

I loved my momma beyond words. I knew I wasn't her favorite, and I knew she and I were very different, but I loved her, and I understood, in ways that Wesley never would, how strong and tough she had needed to be. If Mr. Stancil wanted to marry her, well, I hoped she'd do it; she deserved somebody who thought the world of her.

I looked at Aunt Doris and answered her.

"I think it's great."

She smiled at me as I stood up and walked toward the living room, calling over my shoulder, "Hey Grammie...wanna hear 'Beulah Land'?"

10

It took almost the whole month of April for Aunt Doris to sew the right new dress for Grammie and a new two-piece silk shantung suit for Momma. The first dress she made for Grammie just wouldn't do, so she made another one and then got started on Momma's peach-colored "ensemble," as the pattern read.

Although I had hoped for a new dress myself, I was told that my black linen dress was perfect, and given all the hoopla over this party, I didn't argue. There were shoes and evening bags that had to be dyed to match, undergarments that had to be mended and scrubbed to a fare-thee-well, and hair appointments that had to be scheduled weeks in advance. You'd have thought we were all going to Buckingham Palace.

Miss Bertie had engraved invitations made; they were on fancy, heavy paper, with shiny black ink saying that such and such "is invited to a cocktail buffet followed by a performance by Miss Grace Jeanette Stevens." It gave the date and time and then Miss Bertie's address. Grammie thought it was so fine that she just had to have it framed, so she put hers safely inside the old family Bible until then. Miss Bertie and Aunt Doris had decided not to mention my eighteenth birthday on the invitation, because people would most likely want to bring gifts, and that was not the point.

The two of them, Doris and Bertie El, met or talked on the phone almost daily about the color scheme, the menu, the flowers, and every other detail. Miss Bertie was hiring extra help for that day, because the guest list was up to nearly fifty people. She even arranged to hire an off-duty policeman to help with the parking.

Mr. Stancil insisted that the Buddy Burger close early that day, to insure that he and Momma would be there in plenty of time, dressed to the nines. I let Grammie and Aunt Doris decide who from Mount Vernon Baptist was invited; I knew no matter who did the invitations, somebody was bound to get their feelings hurt. Aunt Doris asked two of her closest office friends, plus DeDee, and I invited six of my high-school gang: Susie, Leslie Joan, Baylin, Jimmy Dale, Gordy, and Hughie. They all came.

Miss Bertie said it would be appropriate to invite Mr. O'Brien, the high-school principal, and my senior advisor, Miss Bingham, who had helped me with all my Vanderbilt paper work, plus I wanted to include Mrs. Bell, my supervisor at the Kress Store.

There were some strays, as Momma called them, that Momma thought should be invited: Edna from the Buddy Burger and Polly; Mr. and Mrs. Thakakis from the diner; Mrs. Adair, our landlord; Grammie's chiropractor, Dr. Hughes; and Lydadelle, a colored lady whom Momma had hired her first day as manager of the Buddy Burger. Wesley, to his undying relief, was excused for the evening to stay at a friend's.

The rest of the guests were people Miss Bertie invited, but little did we know, until that evening, that so many big wheels would be there: the mayor of Grantville; the whole board of trustees of the country club; Edward E. Crocker, the president and CEO of the steel mill; Judge and Mrs. Roberts, John David and Mary Carson Strickland; and several other lawyers and doctors who lived nearby in Riverview Heights. And, of course, nothing like this was going to escape the local newspaper—there was a *Journal* reporter and a photographer out in the driveway.

As you can imagine, it was a great party. It was hands down—no argument, slap out—the fanciest, most elegant thing anyone in my whole family had ever attended. Aunt Doris said afterward that she'd bet her best shoes that even Cynthia Louise Biddle had never seen the like. Miss Bertie had asked Grammie, Aunt Doris, and me to get there early, which was nice—we got to look around and take it all in.

And before the guests arrived, Miss Bertie handed me a white satin box. Inside was the strand of princess-length pearls I had worn in Knoxville.

"I want you to have them, Grace. They look much better on you than they ever did on me," Miss Bertie said with a big grin. Again, she fastened the gold clasp as Aunt Doris just stood there, wide-eyed and mute.

"Happy birthday, dear," Miss Bertie said just as the doorbell rang; before I could even speak, she turned and was walking briskly to the front door.

The dining-room table was covered in an antique lace tablecloth that nearly took Grammie's breath away. A huge arrangement of fresh spring flowers, all in pink and white, cascaded beautifully from a large crystal punch bowl elevated in the center of the long table. There were silver forks and trays and gleaming chaffing dishes beneath the soft light from the dazzling chandelier. Grammie was right, it looked like something out of a magazine.

The food was what Aunt Doris called gourmet—prime beef fillets, exotic cheeses, and artisan breads, flown in especially from New York, and mounds of fresh fruit. I ate, and I'm sure it was all delicious, but to tell you the truth, I didn't really taste anything I put in my mouth. I was too busy looking around.

There was Mrs. Holderness, talking to Grammie about pound-cake recipes; there was Mr. Crocker, talking to Aunt Doris, telling her that he had no idea she had worked in purchasing for the last fourteen years; and there was Mr. Stancil, head to head with Mr. Thakakis, talking shop. Lydadelle, Mrs. O'Brien, and Dr. Reeves's wife, were laughing together about something. In the corner, the Episcopal priest was holding forth with Brother Robbins from Mount Vernon Baptist, and there was Momma, acting as much like a lady as she possibly could, smiling and chatting with Miss Bertie and probably chompin' at the bit for a Lucky.

To see all those people-- dressed to bury, I tell you-- from different sides of Grantville, whose paths had never crossed or who had probably never spoken even if they had, was amazing. Again, I was floored that it was all because of me, Grace Stevens, taking music lessons.

After dinner everyone found a seat as Miss Bertie brought me up to stand beside her at the piano, which had been tuned by a specialist from Richmond and rolled forward. She told everyone how proud she was of me, how hard I had worked, what an extraordinary talent I was, and that I had received a full music scholarship to Vanderbilt University. At that, everyone oooohed and ahhhhhed and then applauded as I *finally* sat down at that fabulous, gleaming black piano.

It would sound silly and childish for me to go on and on about that piano, like it was something magical, but believe me when I tell you this: I played for nearly forty minutes, five pieces in all, and I was more absorbed in what I was doing than I had ever been before. Call me crazy, but I can't help believing it was because of that piano.

Never had I ever heard sounds like that. The depth and resonance of every note was extraordinary. By the time I was halfway through my first sonatina I thought, in a flash, that Chopin and Mozart and Schubert—all of them—would be pea green with envy, because nothing they'd ever heard was as fine as this. They could never have imagined such an instrument, could never have *dreamed* the sound of their music held such richness. Miss Bertie's prized piano was everything I thought it would be and more.

I finished with my favorite, Mozart's "Turkish March," and I knew then that nothing I would ever play on again—no Steinway, no Baldwin, no nothing—could ever compare to that piano, that glistening, *perfect* work of art. I suddenly understood why it meant so much to Miss Bertie, and I felt honored.

As I rose from the bench, I couldn't help myself—I reached out with both my hands and stroked the top of the piano. I wanted to feel the warmth and strength of it, to touch the wood and maybe catch the very last of the vibrations from its mysterious, beautiful insides. It was hard for me to let it go, to remove my hands and just walk away, but I knew I had to.

Although Momma, in her pretty new suit, and Grammie, in her blue satin dress, and Aunt Doris, wearing her mint-green cocktail shift, were all beaming and clapping for me, it was Miss Bertie whose eyes I could feel on me. I looked up, toward the living-room arch where she stood. Sure enough, she was staring at me.

This time she wasn't clapping. She stood perfectly still and erect, her hands clasped ladylike together in front of her as she focused completely on me. Our eyes locked for a long moment, and I thought for a split second that there really, truly must be a special connection between us. I smiled and, a little self-consciously, touched the strand of pearls she had given me.

And then she did it—Miss Bertie gently nodded her head at me. Yes, she was telling me yes. Yes? I wondered, yes *what*? I wouldn't know for many years what she was trying to tell me that night.

Before the evening was over, a large, three-layer birthday cake, with eighteen pink candles, was rolled into the foyer, and everyone lifted crystal flutes of French champagne into the air as they sang "Happy Birthday" to me. It was the first champagne I'd ever tasted, and it was, obviously, the best birthday I'd ever had.

But, as Momma often said, there's always somebody determined to toss a turd in the punch bowl, no matter what. In this case, it was people Miss Bertie knew well.

~୨

Once all the details of the "fete for Miss Stevens" were published in the society section of the *Grantville Journal*, complete with a picture of me, Momma, and Miss Bertie standing with the mayor, the huffin' and puffin' and the "why- I- nevers" began.

Apparently some of Miss Bertie's Women's Auxiliary buddies and some of her bridge-club ladies and even some people at her church were shocked, and others were appalled, that Bertie El would "cross the line" like that. Having mill-village people and Greek immigrants and colored people and Baptists and waitresses and salon girls—*in her home for God's sake*—was evidently beyond the pale to some of them.

One old biddy wondered aloud, "Who does Bertie El Hewitt think she is, bringin' down Grantville's social sets like they're the walls of Jericho?" It was just *not* a good idea.

Miss Bertie kept quiet and went on about her business, but the next opportunity she got with each group, she had her say. Aunt Doris heard all about it, and so did Lydadelle, because, as we'd later come to find out, she was a distant cousin to Evelyn, Miss Bertie's help.

And it even got back to Dr. Garrison, the town's only surgeon, who went home and told his wife to zip it before she and those other Auxiliary pea-hens caused the hospital to lose a hefty upcoming Hewitt donation. Mrs. Garrison's help, Mary Alice, told Evelyn that the doctor said, "It's a free country, Barbara, and Bertie El Hewitt can invite whoever she jolly well pleases into her house...and you need to *stay out of it.*"

Miss Bertie drafted a letter of resignation to every last membership she had to everything in Grantville, and one by one, she stood right up and offered it to them, since they apparently had such bitter objections to her guests...and she made it clear, by insinuation only, that she would be taking her checkbook with her.

Aunt Doris laughed out loud as she told how *that* put an end to it right there. There were, indeed, a couple of resignations, but they *weren't* Miss Bertie's.

The rest of May flew by. Our senior class got to go on an overnight to Chattanooga by bus. We toured the Lookout Mountain battlefield. We went to Rock City. We rode the Incline, and we had a big spaghetti dinner in a private banquet room at the Holiday Inn. And, yes, as soon as I saw the sign for the Chattanooga city limits, I thought about Myra Meyerson, bless her heart.

Jimmy Dale got a new, used Chevelle for graduation, and on the bus ride, he asked me if he could come help me move into the dorm at Vanderbilt, and I said that would be really good.

Although my Vanderbilt scholarship was public knowledge after the party, Miss Bingham still made a special announcement about it at graduation. I was asked to play something, and Miss Bertie suggested that my Mendelssohn sonata would be very nice, which was fine by me.

A week before the ceremony, she even called the school to make sure the old piano in the auditorium would be tuned and well lighted.

So there was another newspaper photo clipping for Grammie: me in my cap and gown, playing Mendelssohn. Wesley said I looked like a date for the main character of *The Nutty Professor*.

I worked most of the summer at the Kress store. I managed to buy myself an inexpensive four-piece vinyl luggage set from Miller's, and Mr. Stancil dug an old footlocker out of his basement and gave it to Momma for me.

It seemed like Aunt Doris sewed day and night; if she wasn't at work in the mill office, she was at her sewing machine. She said I was the family's first college co-ed and that I was going to have the right wardrobe for it if it was the last thing she ever did. I have to say, I left Grantville in September with some gorgeous shirtwaist dresses, wool skirts, and culottes, with matching sweaters, a blazer, and a really nice London Fog raincoat. Aunt Doris said I ought to put on that string of pearls Miss Bertie gave me and wear them with everything!

In September Momma and Aunt Doris drove me to Nashville on a Sunday; well, actually they drove a carload of my stuff, including one of Grammie's pound cakes wrapped in double aluminum foil. Jimmy Dale and I followed in his red Chevelle.

The night before we left, Grammie made my favorite dinner, and just as the five of us sat down together for my "last supper," as Wesley called it, the doorbell rang. To our surprise, in walked Miss Bertie and

Mrs. Holderness; they were all dressed up and on their way to a fund-raiser at the country club and just wanted to stop by quickly.

Grammie, in a soiled apron, which she snatched off her waist like a dead rattlesnake, asked them in.

"Please...y'all come on in....let's sit in the parlor."

In the kitchen, Momma and Aunt Doris rushed around to pour some glasses of iced tea and dump some cinnamon pecans into a little dish. Aunt Doris carried the tray in, while Momma ran to the bathroom to use some Listerclear; thanks to R. T., she had gotten very conscious of having "tobacco breath."

The pork chops and coleslaw were left on the table, and Wesley went to sit on the back porch with a comic book.

Mrs. Holderness immediately commented on the Baldwin, saying how nice it looked and how happy she was that it was being used. They sat down on the sofa, and I went to the piano bench to sit.

From her raggedy recliner, Grammie was chatting about the weather and how it sure was nice to have some cooler nights coming soon. Miss Bertie, who looked as if she had lost weight, reached into her handbag and pulled out an envelope; Mrs. Holderness waited a second or two and then did the same thing.

Aunt Doris sat the tray down on the coffee table and pulled up the ottoman to sit on. A second later, Momma appeared and just stood in the doorway, trying to look pleasantly surprised.

"Grace, tomorrow's the big day, isn't it?" Miss Bertie said, smiling at me.

"Yes, ma'am...it sure is." I nodded.

Grammie, still struggling with the whole thought of me going three hundred miles away, started tearing up.

"Oh...I just don't know what I'm gonna do without her," she mumbled.

Aunt Doris, looking hard at Grammie, tried to call her off. "Momma," was all she said, but the look on her face said "For Lord's sake, don't start again."

"I know it, Mrs. Stevens...we're all going to miss her so much, but she's going to have a wonderful time," Miss Bertie said. "And we're all so proud of her."

Then Aunt Doris jumped in.

"And it's only a four-hour drive, and she'll be back for Thanksgiving before you know it." She was obviously trying to buck-up Grammie.

"So..." Miss Bertie reached and took the envelope from Mrs. Holderness and then handed them both to me. "Laura and I just wanted to drop off a little something for you...to use for books or extras, or whatever...and to tell you to do your best and to stay in touch."

Aunt Doris gasped slightly.

"Bertie El...y'all *shouldn't* have...you've done enough," Aunt Doris said sincerely.

From the doorway, Momma finally spoke.

"Ain't that the gospel truth if I've ever heard it!" she said a little too loudly. "There's already no way I can ever come close to payin' back all you've—"

Miss Bertie cut Momma off.

"Arlene"—Miss Bertie held up her hand toward Momma—"believe me, there's always two sides to everything. What I've done for Grace... well...it's been returned to me many times over in ways you can't imagine. I needed to learn some things...and to be reminded of some other things." She paused as if she didn't really want to go into it.

"Let's just say, I got very, very lucky the day Grace Stevens walked into my life." Miss Bertie looked at me and smiled softly.

At that, Grammie just busted-out blubbering and pulled a wadded-up hankie out of her pocket. Laura Holderness reached over and patted Miss Bertie, and Aunt Doris just grinned.

Momma, leaning against the doorway with her arms folded, looked from Miss Bertie to me; she had an expression on her face that I'd seen before, like she wasn't really sure who I was.

When Miss Bertie and Mrs. Holderness stood up, Aunt Doris and I did, too. Wrapping her arms around me, Miss Bertie hugged me firmly.

"Good luck, Gracie...take care of yourself, and do your best."

I looked her straight in the eyes.

"I will...and thank you so much," I said, and I meant it from the bottom of my heart.

Suddenly we heard the back screen door squeak open and then slam shut. Wesley yelled toward the living room.

"CAN I EAT?"

11

~

To tell you the truth, I've been tempted to leave out a bunch of what happened while I was at Vanderbilt, but if I'm gonna tell the truth, I need to tell it all I guess—guts, feathers and eyeballs.

As you know, college is a big turning point for everybody, one way or another, and God knows, it was for me. Yes, I did finally get a degree, but let's just say I took a little detour that got bumpy. From that rough ride, I gained some insight into myself, and the world, that I badly needed. Would I have eventually gotten it anyway, whether or not I'd gone to college? I don't know. But perspective is a jewel, and I'm not sure just how long it would have taken me to find that shining nugget if I'd just stayed in Grantville.

So let me get on with it.

I'll begin by telling you this; I truly believe that somebody ought to write a book about what happens to kids their first year in college, regarding one thing in particular—roommates. I believe for a fact that whenever a smart, capable kid packs up and goes back home after their first or second semester of college, it's got something to do with a roommate.

Being away from home for the first time is hard enough; learning your way around a campus and a dorm adds to that, but then you throw in some wacky weirdo roommate who a kid has nothing in common with, and there's your formula: unless something changes, somebody's leavin', one way or another. I'm willing to bet that most college graduates can count on one hand the number of people they've ever heard of who liked, much less became friends with, their freshman roommate. There must be some kind of diabolical roommate wheel in the housing office that some clown spins just for fun.

Anyway, so here I was, a little hick from East Tennessee, who knew nobody—*NOBODY*- I'm tellin' you. And who did they put me in the room with but this skinny, stringy-haired girl from Chicago. You heard me, *Chicago*.

Leila Cohen came to Vanderbilt because her father *told* her she was going to Vanderbilt. He also told her that she needed to go be around some "normal" American kids, who were too busy attending parties and football games to be interested in protesting anything. Looking back, I at least stood an outside chance of eventually fitting in somewhere at Vanderbilt; Leila stood no chance.

She dressed like a poor gypsy or somebody who got lost in a Salvation Army store and decided to just put on anything they could snatch-up—long, ugly skirts; dark, thick sandals; tacky, old blouses; and so many strands of beads and trinkets you couldn't count them. Leila did not shave her legs or under her arms; she said bras and makeup were just inventions to suppress natural womanhood, and she said it was only a matter of time before the "movement" arrived in the South.

Apparently, there were several of these "movements" already goin' strong in Chicago, which Leila said were headed our way to Tennessee and would apparently change everything.

In the meantime, Leila stuck out like a stinkweed right in the middle of a bunch of long-stem, all-American red roses.

Those *roses* were the rich, beautiful, perfectly groomed, completely fabulous sorority girls of Vanderbilt University. They were Chi-Os, and Tri-Delts,, and Pi-Phis, and K-Ds. They wore heavy, gold monogrammed jewelry; they dressed like Rich's models; they drove Cutlasses and Mustangs and cute, little convertible Volkswagens, and they stuck together. They all seemed to have grown-up playing tennis, water-skiing, and riding horses. With various fraternities, the sororities hosted hayrides, dances, house parties, teas, and football bashes. Some of the sisters had grandmothers and mothers and aunts and older sisters who had been in the same sorority, and they knew exactly *what* was important and *who* was important at Vandy.

You can imagine what they thought of Leila Cohen and vice versa.

I was lost.

My main goal every time I walked out of my dorm room was to not draw any attention to myself. Mostly, I didn't speak. I didn't make eye contact, and I kept my distance from almost everybody. I found out later that some people thought I was stuck up, which made me laugh out loud. To avoid being lumped in with the "hippy girl from up north," I went out of my way to always look my best, which was nothing special—believe me—compared to all the sorority sisters. Surely, I hoped, people could plainly see that I was nothing like my roommate.

Leila's music—hard, mean-soundin' stuff that was just garbage to me—at times hummed from her stereo until dawn. She draped huge paisley scarves over the light fixtures and burned candles and incense every evening; I figured it was only a matter of time before the whole third floor of our dorm went up in flames. Her side of our room had dark posters of Haight-Ashbury, radical politicians, and occult stuff. Needless to say, I never asked to play any of my Lettermen or Temptations records on her stereo.

To say I was miserable is just not sufficient. I lay awake at night sometimes, wondering what the devil I was doing there. Some mornings when I woke up, the thought of facing another day in this skewed, foreign world would send me fleeing to the showers, where I'd just stand, choking back tears while the water poured over my head. How, in the name of John Brown, was I going to make it through four years of *this*?

I was taking only one music course that first semester—music theory, which was a cakewalk for me given what Miss Bertie had already taught me. Luckily, that course allowed me to reserve one of the practice rooms in the Music Department, and that practice room became my refuge. There was a ninety-minute limit for everybody except seniors, but I stayed as long as I could—either until someone else showed-up or the maintenance man told me the building was closing for the night. I played some of my music. I studied in there. I sometimes ate in there, and I would certainly have probably tried to sleep in there if I'd thought I could get away with it.

Homesick and depressed, going back to that tiny dorm room to see what Vanderbilt's own flower-child, earth-mother Yankee radical was up to filled me with dread. When Thanksgiving break came, I had never in my young life been so happy to see our little garage apartment.

I never said a word about it to my family. They were so proud of me and so impressed with my descriptions of college life, I could have told them that I knew for a fact that my roommate was an ax murderer and they would have simply told me to "just keep an eye on her." After only three months away from home, I now dwelled in a different world, a world they couldn't imagine. How could I tell them that my homemade skirts and Miller's Discount shoes couldn't come close to what most of Vandy's co-eds wore?

Momma and Aunt Doris took me to the bus station on that Sunday morning in November, handed me a brown bag holding a turkey sandwich and a slice of pecan pie, and kissed me good-bye.

"We'll see you in just a few weeks, Gracie," Aunt Doris said.

I smiled and waved from my window seat. Then, as soon as the Greyhound turned the corner, I started to cry. I cried all the way to the other side of Knoxville.

But my deliverance from roommate hell was not far away.

Leila Cohen returned to Vanderbilt after Thanksgiving, with two bags of marijuana, stuff I had never seen or smelled, much less ever smoked. Leila's friends from her political-science class, three long-haired boys and one scroungy-lookin' girl, began to sit around outside under the trees behind the dorm at night, smokin', gigglin', and doin' headstands while they shared big boxes of Cheez-Its.

Of course in hindsight, what they were doing was mild compared to the way things were just a little later, but for Vanderbilt University back then, they were out of control. It did not take long for the campus police to be alerted by our dorm mother that a "weird smell" was drifting through the air at the back of the dorm. Evidently, it had not occurred to Leila and her radicals that her incense and candles might have come in handy out there.

I got back to the dorm from my music cell late one night to find the campus police in our room. They asked me some questions and casually looked through my side of the room—the side without the weird scarves and black-light posters and candles.

Everyone confirmed for them that I had never been seen anywhere in that dorm or on that campus near Miss Leila Miriam Cohen. I realized then that some people understood my bad luck, my random roommate misfortune, in having been paired with the "hippy Yankee girl."

Leila Cohen went to jail for a few days; then she went back to Chicago after her dad came and hired some attorneys. Then I had the dorm room all to myself for the rest of the semester, until Christmas break. For the first time in my life, I had my own room. I got a taste of privacy, and it was heaven.

In January, I returned to Vandy and to a new roommate, a special roommate that became a remarkable friend I'll never forget. How I, Grace Stevens, wound up rooming with the most popular girl in the freshmen class, I'll never know, but there it is.

Ellis Anne Hammonds, from Hammondsville in north Georgia, was already well known at Vandy even before she'd stepped out of her daddy's Lincoln back in September to begin her freshman year. Ellis Anne's older brother, Tommy, was a senior and president of the Sigma Nu fraternity at Vanderbilt, so there were plenty of people who were already well aware of Tommy's little sister, whom some people called E. A. for short.

Within three months of that September day, *everybody* knew who Ellis Anne Hammonds was; she was named the freshmen representative to the homecoming queen's court; she was first runner-up in the Miss Vanderbilt fall pageant, and she was chosen by the dean's office as an official Commodore hostess, an honor normally reserved only for junior and senior girls.

Despite all this, the biggest heartbreak for Ellis Anne was the fact that she could not be rushed for a sorority until the end of her freshman year—it was a restriction that Vanderbilt enforced. It was also a rule that no sorority member was eligible to live in her sorority house until junior year.

After the holidays, I went back for my second semester, figuring there was no way I would keep my third-floor, end-of-the-hall room all to myself—and I figured right. Ellis Anne's fall roommate had quit school after one semester to go home and get married, so Ellis was moved up to the third floor to room with me.

She had just returned from spending Christmas and New Year at her family's beach house on the coast of South Carolina, and she was just thrilled to be back at school, because she was being rushed in the spring by Chi O, the same sorority that her aunt Melody had pledged. So do you get the picture? I went from one roommate extreme to the other in less than thirty—count 'em—thirty little days.

Ellis Anne was a short, blond cutie whose unbelievable bust line had put her in the "bombshell" category by the time she was fifteen years old. Her bosom was every young man's dream and every dress-maker's nightmare, I'm sure. With a suntan, long golden hair, big brown eyes, a tiny waist, and those tits, Ellis Anne was well on her way to leaving a memorable mark on Vanderbilt. Eventually we all realized that she was basically north Georgia's answer to Dolly Parton.

Truthfully, things worked out well between us right from the get-go. E. A. and I became friends, mainly because despite her family's money and her spoiled, prissy, Daddy's girl upbringing and her complete disinterest in anything academic, there was not a snobby, conceited bone in her body.

Ellis Anne was so thoroughly consumed with what she was going to wear next, who was going to ask her to the SAE's Valentine dance, and how she could explain to her daddy that she had overdrawn her checking account *again*—already—she was not at all upset with who I was, how I got to Vandy, or where I had come from. On her new stereo, we played my Lettermen albums and her Petula Clark records, and we talked for hours about makeup and hair and fashion and boys and dream houses and jewelry.

The biggest problem in that dorm room became Ellis Anne's clothes—where to put them all. After filling her own closet, she used part of mine. Then she hung stuff on a rack behind the door; she overloaded all her drawers and finally resorted to some boxes that we somehow managed to stuff beneath our beds. There were clothes and shoes and coats and fancy lingerie everywhere...I couldn't imagine how one person could possibly wear so much, but I soon learned that Ellis Anne's momma had trained her to never, *ever*, be seen in the exact same outfit more than once. She said "coordinating and accessorizing" were the keys.

Watching E. A. get dressed for a date was a production that often drew a crowd to our room. And that's when I began to meet some other girls and really enjoy living in a big freshman dorm.

There was no studying in that dorm room, so if I really had to get something done, I went over to the Music Department or downstairs to one of the little sitting rooms off the dorm's main parlor.

Don't ask me how, but Ellis Anne somehow squeaked through and always managed to pass her tests. After all, her sorority future hinged on her GPA; her goal was simply to stay in school and make good enough grades to become a Chi Omega, have an unending whirlwind of a social life, and then to wind up married to a Vanderbilt doctor or lawyer. If she got a degree fine; if not, that was fine, too.

Many mornings I just shook my head and went on to class while E. A. rolled over and went back to sleep.

As expected, by early May three different sororities were vying for Ellis Anne, but just as she had said, Vanderbilt's Chi Omega Chapter was her choice, and she was theirs, first and foremost.

By the end of rush, probably 75 percent of the freshmen girls had pledged a sorority, leaving the rest of us on our own. We were either too ugly or too poor—and that's the hard, cold truth—to be part of campus Greek life. I was lucky enough, at least, to be in that latter category.

I assumed that E. A. would make plans to room with one of her fellow Chi O pledges just as soon as she possibly could, and I was saddened at the thought that she and I probably wouldn't remain friends; plus I'd soon be trying to adjust to another roommate. But...surprise, surprise... Ellis Anne announced to a group of three other new Chi Os, gathered in our room one afternoon, that she had no intention of rooming with anybody else but her "dear, sweet Grace."

From across the room, where I was folding my laundry and minding my own non-sorority business, I heard her and turned around. E. A. was looking at me with a big smile on her face.

I just stood there—staring back at her, thinking that she was joking or suddenly being a smartass or something.

But on the other hand, it crossed my mind, at some deep, hurt-filled spot, that maybe I hadn't given her enough credit; maybe somewhere beneath all her self-absorption and her new sorority sisterhood, she had realized how left-out I felt, how a wide, pricey gap now stretched between the two of us, and that her world was now in an orbit far beyond mine.

I say this because there is just no telling what kind of look I had on my face; the next thing I knew, E. A. was hugging me and telling her Chi O sisters that "This girl right here is my very, very best friend!"

That declaration probably caused some of the girls in that dorm and on that campus to question Ellis Anne Hammonds's good sense; after all, the whole point in joining a sorority was to have a special, preset group of girlfriends with whom you did *everything*—exclusively. Wasn't that why they were called sisters?

But evidently if the popular, beautiful, fashionable Miss Hammonds of Hammondsville, Georgia, said that her very best friend at Vanderbilt was *not* a sorority sister, then so be it. Who in their right mind was going to tell Tommy Hammonds, president of Sigma Nu, that his little sister couldn't be friends with anybody she damn well pleased? So, you get the picture...if E. A. Hammonds had declared me the next face of Betty

Crocker or the first woman in space right then and there, it would have stood, unquestioned.

We--Grace Stevens and Ellis Anne Hammonds--remained roommates and friends, and as far as I knew, nobody—Chi O or otherwise—was going to tell E. A. any different.

Now, let me just explain something right now: I did not join a sorority at Vanderbilt. I never had the money or the clothes or the car or, quite honestly, the confidence. And I know what you're thinking—how could somebody who could perform a Chopin concerto on a stage in front of hundreds of people lack confidence? Well, all I can tell you is that feelings of inferiority are powerful, and although they might eventually fade for some of us, they may never totally disappear.

So while I never became a Chi O, there were plenty of people who figured I might as well have been one. Because of E. A. I was like a fringe member, and I'm sure—in fact I know—several of the sisters did not like it at all. But what could they do? Ellis Anne Hammonds went right from being a freshman phenom to a sophomore phenom, and yes, we roomed together our second year at Vandy.

E. A. returned to Vandy that second September driving a solid white 1969 Chevrolet T-top Corvette with white leather interior. Her daddy had to follow her to Nashville, hauling all her boxes and suitcases of clothes and shoes in Mrs. Hammonds's station wagon. From in front of the Student Union Building, Mr. Hammonds hired two boys to haul all of it to our third-floor room. Afterwards he left, handing Ellis Anne a wad of money as she kissed him good-bye at the door.

I had worked two jobs that summer—one at the Kress and then part time at the Buddy Burger, and with Aunt Doris's help, I had managed to improve and expand my wardrobe. We had shopped in Knoxville twice that summer, and Aunt Doris had splurged on several Vogue patterns for me. Ellis Anne had invited me down to her family's beach house for a week in July, but I had made-up some excuse about needing to be at home to help with my grandmother, which wasn't a little white lie—it was a big, fat whopper.

Besides working that summer, I visited regularly with Miss Bertie. She seemed different to me, but, of course, everybody seemed different to me. As always, she was so good to me and was eager to hear about everything; every single thing I could think of about my first year of college, she wanted to hear about. And, of course, we talked about music, and we had chicken salad and ice tea as we listened to some of her new albums.

By the fall of my second year at Vandy, I was feeling a lot more comfortable, especially over in the music building. Sometimes in the late afternoon, some of us music majors would sit around in the common area of the rehearsal rooms and talk, mostly about music and various professors. The group shared all kinds of interests—everything from classical to jazz to bluegrass to the Beatles. Looking back on that now, I realize how wonderful those sessions were and how much I learned.

There was a five-piece jazz group that would sometimes jam at night in one of the rooms, and one afternoon their lead bass player stopped me in the hall. He said their pianist had fractured his hand playing flag football and they needed someone to rehearse a new version, "groove" he called it, of the "Tennessee Waltz" they were working up. Would I help them out for the next week or so?

I quickly answered that I knew nothing—nada—about jazz piano, but he quickly said I could pick it up in no time and that Chuck, their pianist, would help me.

Now believe me, of all the versions you have ever heard of the "Tennessee Waltz," there is no way to describe the one that group did. It started out all slow and traditional and then wham! The whole thing exploded into a rockin', rollin', boogie-woogie, hit-the-roof, jump-and-jive swing number. And to my surprise, I did pick it up, and boy, was it fun.

It was a jolt to practice my classical pieces, work on my piano theory, and then, ten minutes later, walk into that setting. I was once again amazed at the piano—how an instrument could give life to Mozart and then turn right around and rock out with a bass, two horns, and drums to a jazzy ballad was still remarkable to me. It was so good and so much fun I didn't even let myself think of what Miss Bertie would have said.

Well, helping out that little jazz group was not only a great new experience, it also opened a new door for me. Since two of those guys were members of the Alpha Tau Omega fraternity, the next thing I knew, I was invited to a party at the ATO house the night before the Ole Miss game.

E. A. squealed. No, I guess she actually *shrieked* when I told her that I had been officially invited to an ATO party. Of course, she was already invited, since the Chi O sisters had a standing invitation to all the stag fraternity parties. The big dances and the balls and the house parties were a different story, but just a general Friday night, run-of-the-mill frat party was no big deal—except to someone like me, who would never have crossed the threshold of *any* fraternity house without a specific invitation.

E. A. saw this as a great turning point for me, and if I'd had any sense, I would have seen it that way, too, but for a totally different reason.

12

~

By then I was nineteen years old, and other than the glass of champagne at my eighteenth birthday party and a glass of Chianti two different times in an Italian restaurant in downtown Nashville, I had no experience with serious, abandoned, let's-get-wasted, knee-walkin'-drunk consumption of alcohol. That September E. A. had come in late at night, tipsy and giggling, a few times, feeling much freer to do so now that her older brother was no longer at Vandy keeping strict watch over her. But at that point, drinking did not interest me. Unfortunately, that changed.

Purple Jesus—that's what they called it. In big, aluminum washtubs, they poured tall cans of grape juice and/or Hawaiian Punch and either straight-grain alcohol or the cheapest vodka that could be bought. If anyone was motivated enough, there might occasionally be slices of oranges or lemons floating around in the stuff, and sometimes I think someone may have poured some ginger ale or 7 Up or even orange juice into the brew.

There was no exact recipe, because once someone had a Dixie cup or two of the stuff, the taste just didn't matter. The ATOs called it purple Jesus, but it was also called jungle juice or hunch punch. Whatever it was called, it was damn near lethal.

That night at the ATO house, I did something that I would never have done in a gazillion years had I not been on my third cup of purple Jesus—I sat down at the old, shabby, beat-up baby grand in the living room of the ATO house, and I played—no, I blew-out—that jazz take of the "Tennessee Waltz."

By the time I was nearly finished, there was a crowd of people around me, hootin' and hollerin', cheerin' and beggin' me not to stop. Finally, after I was breaking into a sweat, I ended with a flashy, showy, Jerry-Lee-Lewis glissando that bowled them over. Then I hopped- up on the piano bench and took a long bow to the applause, as some guy handed me another cup of that sweet, fruity magic.

Miss Bertie would have been horrified, but right then she and Grantville hardly existed for me; that life, before Vandy, faded into a happy, distant fog with every sip I swallowed.

Now where else-- other than from drinking that purple stuff-- would I have ever found that kind of ballsy audacity? It was like I was somebody else altogether, I tell you. I was laughin' and struttin' around like a new Grace Stevens—someone who was anything but a simple scholarship student from a family living in a garage apartment, without so much as the proverbial pot, attending college on a shoestring and wearing homemade clothes. Purple Jesus wiped all that out—every last bit of it—and that night I had a blast.

So that's how it started. I don't know what else to tell you, other than just imagine drinking something from a paper cup that made you feel, for the first time in your life, that a whole new, untapped, extraordinary part of yourself had been unwrapped? That made you feel like the strings or the tape had been ripped right-off your mummified-self and out stepped this bold, confident edition of someone you hadn't known was even in there?

I guess after that night, I figured that drinking was a great way—perhaps my only way—to fit- in, to feel like I *belonged* at Vanderbilt, with all those well-to-do fraternity and sorority kids who did not seem to have a care in the world. Or maybe drinking just numbed the deep-down, nagging doubt I felt from thinking that I'd never fit-in, not really, not in a million years.

So with the help of purple Jesus, and several other strange liquid discoveries, I constructed a new persona of myself, and get this—you'll really get a hoot out of this—I was very proud of the fact that I never, *ever*, drank beer or whiskey. Never.

Those two items I assigned, totally, to my daddy. In those familiar containers and those exact smells were the very liquid embodiments of some of my worst childhood memories, and I hated them. Nope...I was not about to sink that low, I told myself. Beer and whiskey were for losers, and I disliked even smelling it on anybody, which could have been a problem, since most of the frat boys lived on beer, but, hey, I was not dating anyone anyway.

Now how's that for a twisted, naïve rationale?

I actually convinced myself that as long as I wasn't drinking beer or whiskey, I was in the clear and that things would be just fine. So that's what being nineteen years old and stepping off into a snake pit will get you, I guess. I was nineteen, and I couldn't—as they say---see the forest for the trees.

The official partying was kept mostly to the weekends, but once I was in the loop, it wasn't hard to find some place to go any night of the week, and there was always someone asking me to "just go over there for a little while." That "while" was never little, which meant I woke-up some mornings feeling like death eatin' a cracker, and either dragged myself to class or didn't bother to go at all.

I started living on TAB diet drinks, Fritos, and Excedrin, because I couldn't, or didn't, bother to make it to the cafeteria for meals.

By mid-November, my grades were dropping; I was in danger of flunking chemistry, which would have meant the end of my scholarship. But God Almighty, I was having fun almost nonstop...drunken, silly, laugh-my-ass-off fun almost every night.

The F on my chemistry midterm did get my attention; I stood outside the Math-Sci Building and stared at my test booklet long and hard. On the back page, my chemistry instructor had scribbled a note in bright red ink:

Miss Stevens, if you have any intention of passing this course, you need to get some help.

Addiction, I'm not sure I had ever even heard the word.

Growing up, the most I had ever heard was that somebody—and it was most often a man—was "bad to drink" or that "the bottle's got him for sure" or "that poor girl married a boozer."

Actually, I thought there were basically just two kinds of men: men like my daddy, who drank, and men like the preachers and church deacons, who didn't drink. The first group certainly outnumbered the second group on the side of Grantville where my family lived.

And as for women drinking, regularly drinking...well, I couldn't really imagine it; my momma drinking a cold beer maybe once a year was just about more than Grammie and Aunt Doris could live with. I knew, of course, that there were honky-tonk hussies, with bleached hair and tight sweaters, who drank, but I had only ever seen them at a distance, since they weren't exactly regulars at Mount Vernon First Baptist.

And the word alcoholic? Again, it was something I just didn't hear.

I realized later that kids like me and Wes and our friends were mostly shielded and protected from the hard truths of full-blown alcoholism that surely existed in Grantville, as it does everywhere. But people didn't talk about things like that back then; people tried to hide and cover- up, not wanting the whole town knowing the shame and embarrassment of their sad, personal business. People kept their dirty laundry hidden.

And that's exactly why I didn't have the first idea that my daddy, Hoyt Stevens, was the son of one of the meanest, most legendary drunks in East Tennessee.

If there had been terms like "addictive personality traits" and an "alcoholic behavior model" back then, my grandfather, I eventually learned, could have been their original poster boy.

But at the time, how was I to know that all during his young life, his early years as a husband and father, my grandpa Billy not only drank moonshine, he brewed it, ran it across state lines, and sold it. What he couldn't manage to sell, he happily gulped down himself, after which he'd fight anything and anybody who so much as looked at him. Billy

Stevens was known for bustin' heads and smashin' mouths with every-body from federal agents to deputy sheriffs to his best friends and even his own wife and kids. Liquor, they said, turned him into the very devil, because, people believed, he had that Cherokee blood in him.

"Hell," they'd snicker, "even the US government knows a damn Indian can't handle firewater."

And then one day it all stopped. Nobody ever knew for sure what caused it, but Billy Stevens changed. It was a miracle, they said, that, given the life he had led, "the sumbitch lived to beat the bottle." By the time I was born, Grandpa Billy had long since seen the light, quit drinking, and never had another drop. He was, at last, what Grammie said he was: "Finally fit to live with."

But all that came too late for his son. By sixteen, Hoyt's definition of manhood, and his very identity, were both rooted in drinking beer and store-bought whiskey, moonshine hooch having all but died out. Young Hoyt Stevens learned early, at the knee of a master, that enough alcohol boosted confidence, spawned courage and bravado, entertained and distracted, and, of course, numbed all the pain-- be it physical or emotional.

I wouldn't find out until much later that my memories of Momma arguing with Daddy over his hours at the Cozy Corner were nothing—couldn't come close—to the horror of some of Daddy's memories, memories of a childhood stunted by an irrational, rampaging drunk of a father. Once I was told, it all made perfect sense to me—how my daddy had never had any use at all for people who claimed they were *reformed*.

"Reformed my ass," he'd say, because he knew the damage couldn't be undone or "reformed."

But in my sophomore year at Vandy, I was still in the dark about all this. I had no idea that a familial freight train of dynamite was headed right smack toward me, and that no amount of music lessons or college courses or money, for that matter, could protect me.

I pulled a D in chemistry that semester—the first D I had ever made in anything. Since my other grades had also dropped, my overall GPA for fall semester landed me on academic probation.

During Christmas vacation, I tap-danced my way through a believable explanation for Momma and Aunt Doris—some mumbo-jumbo about getting behind, not understanding chemistry in the first place, and missing some classes because of menstrual cramps. It was all Grade-A bullshit, but they seemed to buy it and told me to buckle-down because another semester like that and I'd lose my scholarship.

Grammie never said a word, but I caught her looking at me hard once or twice. And, of course, more than anyone else, Grammie noticed what kind of music I now often played on my piano; jazz, blues, and pop stuff that she simply referred to as "honky-tonk music."

It was as if Grammie knew something was different and that there was a huge shift in everything about me.

Yes, indeed, things *were* different. The truth was that I couldn't *wait* to get back to Vanderbilt. I couldn't wait to get the hell out of Grantville, and I couldn't wait to walk into the first January fraternity party I could find and start drinking and laughing and dancing and *living* again. Being home now was torture, torture that was squared by the fact that I sometimes felt so guilty.

Oh no, it wasn't the drinking that caused my guilt; uh-uh, the drinking had put me in touch with a whole new part of myself and a whole new world that I thought was just fine. The guilt came from how I now felt about my family and about Grantville.

Suddenly my family irritated me night and day; they were tacky and unsophisticated and out of touch with everything that was new and interesting and cool. They asked stupid questions; they seemed like simpletons and pathetic hillbillies to me. In eighteen short months, my experiences and my high and mighty *college scholarship* had propelled me so far above them that, at some deep level, I just knew for sure that I had left them in the dust.

Yep...I was so impressed with myself that the three women who had worked and scrapped and schemed and sacrificed for me now seemed like losers, naïve hayseeds, to me. *That* is how full of shit I was. How's that for some gratitude?

And Grantville? Oh, I couldn't wait to get the hell out of there...back to Nashville or Knoxville or anywhere. Grantville, the town that I had once dreaded leaving and shed tears for, was now backward and dull. I met a group of my high-school friends at Pasquale's Pizza one night, where they were all pumped at sharing a couple of pitchers of beer. I just sipped my Coke and watched them, thinking, if they only knew—knew about *real* drinking and *real* fun. The holiday break couldn't end fast enough for me.

I was, of course, riding for a fall; nobody gets by with that attitude for very long. But I did get by for a while, and as I got more and more removed from the good sense and discipline and hard work that had defined me up until then, I got deeper and deeper, way over my head, into a life that I once could never have imagined—a place I had no business being and sure didn't really belong.

That cold January morning before I left Grantville, I went by to see Miss Bertie. According to Momma and Aunt Doris, the town gossip was that Bertie El was sick; she had been seeing doctors in Knoxville and in Richmond. Nobody knew any of the details, but there was no doubt Miss Bertie was sick, but she was not going to talk about it or whine about it to anybody. She was noticeably thinner, less feisty and just different somehow.

At the front door of her house, she hugged me and told me that she'd see me in the spring and that by then she expected to see my initial list of music for my senior performance.

"You know, Grace, you're already a sophomore...so in only two years from now, you've got to be ready," she said, smiling at me.

That sounded like an eternity to me; at the moment I was more interested in just getting back to campus for the first party.

⌒ჿ

After that Christmas, I didn't go back to Grantville for over a year-- a whole year plus some, if you can believe it. These were

months—a relatively short stretch of time containing some unfathom-
able events--during which I came very close to completely losing myself
and everything that had been within my reach. Sometimes people just
have to learn things the hard way, and that was exactly what was going
to happen to me.

I got back to Vandy after the holidays, and for a while, the party
circuit died down a bit. With winter set in and the holidays over, things
were relatively quiet compared to fall semester. E. A. and I spent some
Friday nights cruising around in her 'vette, sipping cheap vodka cut
with 7 Up. If we didn't finish a bottle, we'd sneak it into the dorm to
stash it, mainly because I was not about to pour any of that happy elixir
down a drain. E. A. would drink a little, but she mostly could just take it
or leave it; I was the one who looked forward to every drop.

It was fun to feel so relaxed and comfortable, and it was during these
times that E. A. and I became really close, soul-mate-kinda friends. She
listened to all the tacky, pathetic details of my life in Grantville, and I
listened to her bitch and moan about the strict, unforgiving expecta-
tions of being "the Hammondses' daughter." It was often hard for me to
see the downside of her situation, but for her, there were certainly pres-
sures that had always rested on her. "And these tits..." she'd say, gestur-
ing with her hands toward her bosom, "when *they* arrived, it only added
to my load!" We laughed ourselves silly at that pun.

In early March, I got a note from Janelle, the three-hundred-pound
secretary in the Music Department, whom I had never seen when
she *wasn't* eating a Snickers candy bar. I'd heard that a student could
get anything out of Janelle for a couple of Snickers. The note said Dr.
Heller, the department head, wanted to see me at my "earliest conve-
nience," which Janelle interpreted for me as "right damn fast." My Gpa
was OK so far that semester, mainly because I'd dropped Chem II, so I
wondered what this was about; had I screwed up something or what?

It turned out the famous Hermitage Hotel in downtown Nashville
had just had its old grand piano restored and placed in the beautifully
remodeled main lobby of the historic building. They'd called Vanderbilt,
asking if Dr. Heller knew of a Vanderbilt music student who might want

to earn a little extra money for a few hours' work every weekend? They thought it would be lovely to have someone play classical and maybe some easy-listening music on Saturday afternoon and again on Sundays from two to five. They would pay twenty-five dollars.

Hanging up the phone, Dr. H. had looked at Janelle and asked if she had any suggestions, and bless Janelle's heart—and her fat ass—if my name didn't pop immediately into her head, she told me later. And, no, I had never given Janelle a Snickers or so much as a penny Tootsie Roll, but I had always tried to be kind to her, because I actually felt sorry for her. Maybe that mattered—I don't know—but after speaking briefly with Dr. H., I stood in front of Janelle's desk as she called the hotel manager back and gave him my name. It was all set; I was to be there on Saturday at two.

"Now, Grace, don't go down there and start playing that boogie-woogie crap," Janelle said between bites of her Snickers as she scribbled the address down for me, "and wear something plain and simple... performance attire I'd say is your best bet."

She handed me the address, and I nodded my head.

"Hey...thanks, Janelle. I really do appreciate this," I said, trying to sound sincere without being mushy.

"You're welcome, Grace...now knock 'em out, and make us proud," she said, turning back to her typewriter.

Outside the music building, I stopped. Twenty-five dollars every weekend? That was nearly a certified fortune to me.

One thing often leads to another, right? But it's rarely ever without some kind of fallout or blowback and *consequences*—God knows, don't ever forget the consequences.

So I went to work at the Hermitage, but it could hardly be called work, since I sat in a lovely room and played the piano as various well-to-do, well-heeled people glided by, coming and going to Nashville's most famous hotel. I quickly met most of the front-desk staff, plus the bartenders in the main lounge, where I was soon spending all of my ten-minute breaks. Without even asking, I was given something to drink, usually club soda or a Coke, and it was Big Earl, the bar manager, who gave me a large, empty vase one afternoon in early April.

"Here, kid...take this and put it on the edge of your keyboard. You never know...somebody might want to leave you a tip now and then." And Big Earl was right.

It was not unusual for me to leave at five on Saturdays with eight or nine dollars of tips in bills and coins. I was amazed.

Getting to the Hermitage on Saturday and Sunday afternoons was not a problem; E. A. was happy to drop me off, but getting back was not so easy. I could have taken a bus, with one transfer, but I hated that idea, so I started walking four blocks up to a small blues club where one of the ATO horn players worked. I'd sit around in there and usually ride back to campus with him. Nobody got carded in those days, so I could sit at the bar and sip one vodka collins after another, waiting on my ride. Since I was "the horn player's friend" I sometimes drank for free, so do you see how the pieces were just falling into place? I don't think it could have come much easier.

In late April, when spring break arrived, I didn't go home; I went with E. A. to her family's beach house in South Carolina, and that week was an eye-opener, much like my first visits with Miss Bertie years before had been. I splurged and bought myself a sundress, a new swim-suit, and some sassy red sandals to take.

I didn't let on to the Hammonds that I had never seen the ocean-- I just walked right out on that beach and played in the water and lay in the sun as if I'd been doing it all my life. I ate crab and shrimp and snapper fillets like they were going out of style, and I drank. I drank bloody marys with eggs Benedict in the mornings, I drank wine and frozen Daiquiris all afternoon, and then at night there was more wine and fancy cocktails.

And, yes, there was always beer...but not for me. No, siree... I had my standards.

The Hammonds had a colored woman named LaLa...actually her name was Clara, but years ago baby Tommy could only say LaLa, so that was that. LaLa went everywhere the family went, so at the beach LaLa kept everybody in clean beach towels, iced drinks, and the best cheese straws I've ever put in my mouth. She made brunch every day, which we ate on the screened porch, but no other prepared meals, since we had dinner out every night, with LaLa joining us.

That week was like a travel-magazine, hit-the-jackpot dream vacation to me. This, I thought, is the life. That trip was a huge turning point.

I knew after that trip that I wasn't going back to Grantville for the summer. There was just no way.

How could I go back and work at the Kress and the Buddy Burger, sit around at night with Aunt Doris and Grammie, shelling peas and puttin' up tomatoes, and hang-out in that grubby Pasquale's, talking to my old high-school buds who still spoke with terrible grammar and believed in space aliens? I'd go slap-out nuts back there, and I knew it. But, as always, money was the issue.

If money was the question—the determinant for my avoiding a summer back in Grantville—I had to find an answer and find it sooner rather than later. And you can probably guess what the answer was, can't you? It was what it had always been for me, what had already become my ticket out of Grantville—the piano.

At around four thirty on the first Saturday afternoon of May, I looked up from the keyboard and noticed Mr. Gaines, the hotel manager, walking nervously toward me. The Hermitage lobby was busy but not actually crowded yet; since the weather was so nice a lot of people were outdoors, I guess. I finished a sweet version of "A Summer Place" just as he stopped beside me.

"Grace, can you come with me, dear?" he said curtly.

Glancing up at the huge clock on the wall to my left, I was about to point out that I had another half hour left, but he spoke again before I could say a word.

"Don't worry about the time...I need to speak to you in my office," he said, tilting his head in that direction and motioning for me to follow him.

I gathered up my small stack of sheet music and my purse then hurried after him. Maybe he had heard that I'd been having a drink sometimes in the bar before I left. Oh shit, I thought.

Outside his office, there were several other people scurrying; two phones were ringing, and a man from a florist was waving a large clipboard and asking for directions. Mr. Gaines blew past all of that activity, walked straight into his office, and finally stopped behind his desk; he told me to close the door behind me.

"Grace, here's the deal...the Sokol-Weinstein wedding is tonight at Temple Beth El. Do you know who I'm talking about?"

"No, sir," I answered.

He paused and looked at me as if I was a moron.

"Oh...that's right...you aren't from Nashville, are you?"

He didn't even catch his breath before continuing.

"Never mind then...but here's the problem. The reception is here, upstairs in the main ballroom, preceded by drinks and hors d'oeuvres on the balcony before dinner and dancing. Esther Weinstein just called— damn near in cardiac arrest—to say the piano player who was supposed to play before dinner has apparently disappeared. His roommate claims he left town early this morning...who the hell knows...but I assured Mrs. Weinstein that I would find someone for her. So, I'm hoping, Grace, that you can do this. It would help us out enormously, and I think you would probably be paid nicely. What do you say?"

The first thing I thought about, believe it or not, was *not* the money; it was how I looked. Since my black performance dress was in the cleaners, I had worn a short, black corduroy jumper and a beige blouse—not exactly right for some fancy spring wedding. I had on black flats, and there was a run in my panty hose.

Worried at the look on my face, Mr. Gaines went on.

"Grace, it will only be for an hour or so, no more than an hour and a half. The orchestra starts at nine thirty...and you can drink all you want of the imported champagne," he offered, almost with a plea.

"Well...I've got a run in my hose...and—" I began.

He didn't hesitate. From his pocket, he jerked a five-dollar bill and handed it across the desk.

"Here...go buy yourself some hose and a lipstick, and grab a sandwich, too, OK?"

He looked at me, and I knew I couldn't refuse. I nodded my head.

"Oh, Jesus...thank you, Grace." Mr. Gaines smiled with relief, waving me out as he picked up one of his phone lines that had begun ringing.

I took my time and walked all the way downtown to Harvey's, where I bought myself some Hanes panty hose, which I slipped on in the ladies' room on the mezzanine. Then I walked across the street to Woolworth and bought a dark red lipstick and some bobby pins. When I got back to the Hermitage, Phyllis, one of the barmaids, helped me pin up my hair, and then I sat down at the bar and had a vodka collins. Thumbing through my music, I realized that I didn't have enough popular pieces with me; I'd have to improvise my way through "I Left My Heart in San Francisco," "Moon River," and "Never on Sunday." I figured I couldn't exactly play the *Moonlight Sonata* for cocktails.

A little before eight o'clock, Big Earl walked me up the back stairs to the main balcony that overlooked the lobby. I took one look and stopped dead in my tracks; on three long tables were candelabras and flower arrangements that were all at least three feet tall. Five waiters were putting the finishing touches on food that was so beautiful and exotic-looking I couldn't imagine eating any of it. There were stacks of champagne glasses around a bubbling fountain; there were glittering strands of ribbon around the tables, and there were piles of tiny, scallop-edged engraved napkins with an *S* and a *W* entwined.

And way back, almost in the corner, was a baby grand piano, on which someone had placed a large flower arrangement. It was just as well, I thought; the better for me to hide behind and blend into. With all this, the piano music was probably just an afterthought anyway.

"Here she is, Cotton," Big Earl called to one of the waiters, who walked over, wiping his hands on his large apron.

"So you're Grace, right?"

"Yes, sir, I am," I muttered, still looking around.

"Cotton, give this girl a glass of champagne before they all get here," Big Earl suggested as he turned to leave.

"I'll take good care of her, Earl," Cotton said as he spread his arm out toward the piano, motioning me to it.

As it turned out, I had two glasses of champagne and most of a third glass, thanks to one of the other waiters, while I played typical bar/cocktail music, but who cared? The minute the guests started arriving, it got so loud and so crowded I could have been playing "What a Friend We Have in Jesus," and no one would have noticed. As far as I knew no one even saw me there in the corner behind the flowers, and I never saw the bride or the groom or any of the wedding party.

I played until about nine fifteen, when Cotton came over and tapped me on the shoulder.

"Grace, you can finish up...they're about to go into the ballroom."

I nodded my head.

"And this is from Mr. Weinstein." Cotton handed me a twenty-dollar bill.

I smiled and nodded again. This was about the easiest money I'd ever earned.

I slipped away, down the back stairs, and quickly made my way around to the bar. I was a little buzzed and was hoping Big Earl would make me another vodka collins, and I was also wondering how I was going to get back to campus. There's always the bus, I thought. As I sat down on my regular barstool near the side register, Big Earl looked up from the bar sink.

"How'd it go, Gracie?" he asked.

"It was good...but I don't think anyone heard anything I played," I said, shrugging my shoulders and chuckling. At that moment, I realized someone had walked right up behind me, mainly because Big Earl's gaze suddenly shifted. Someone had followed me down the back stairs.

"Oh, I heard you...I heard you just fine, miss. I especially liked your 'Moon River Medley.'"

I turned on the swivel barstool and came face to face, almost nose to nose since he was standing so close, to a young man who nearly took my breath away. I'm sure I literally gasped, or at least my mouth just fell open. In a crazy flash, it occurred to me that if statues of Greek gods could come to life, before me, for sure, was what one would look like.

He was medium height, with dark, curly hair—ringlets, actually—and wide amber-colored eyes with eyelashes that women just wish for. His skin was dark but not from a suntan, just naturally so, and he was wearing a tuxedo with the shirt unbuttoned at the top and the bow tie hanging undone. His hands were jammed down into his pockets, and he was smiling at me.

I couldn't move. Honestly, *I could not move*. I'm sure I sat there like a dunce, unblinking, my mouth agape, and for some reason, I was suddenly stone sober—no buzz, no tipsy lilt, no nothing. I was clear-headed, and my vision was immediately sharp and vivid.

Seeing me in a near catatonic state, Big Earl spoke-up.

"Can I help you, buddy?"

Adonis slid onto the barstool beside me, still smiling.

"Yes, sir...I'd like to buy this lady a beer...and—"

Before he could finish, Earl interrupted.

"She doesn't drink beer," he said a little gruffly, glancing at me now.

"Grace, do you want a collins?"

I finally took a breath and nodded my head toward Earl, without taking my eyes off the mystery god.

Adonis spoke again.

"OK, then a collins it is...and a cold Heineken for me, please."

That is how David Jacob Eisenberg walked into my life.

I probably don't need to tell you how I got back to the dorm that night or that I did *not* go home to Grantville that summer.

13

~

"It's not what you know; it's who you know."

How many times had I heard that? And I knew firsthand that even in a place like Grantville, who I had known had already changed my life. It was about to change again because of that little adage.

From just playing the piano that night at a big Jewish wedding, and subsequently meeting David, I ended up making more money that spring and summer than you'd believe. I played at cocktail parties, bar mitzvahs, more weddings, teas, receptions, graduations—you name it. By the end of May, I had business cards, courtesy of David—three simple lines engraved over the outline of a grand piano:

PIANO GRACE
Miss Grace Stevens
Classical & Popular Music

"I didn't have them put a phone number or address. You can just jot that at the bottom or on the back when you need to, Grace," David said, handing them to me.

I opened the box and took one out and stared. It was a Thursday evening, and we were sitting at our usual table in the bar at the Hermitage. I needed to get back to the dorm to study for finals, but I was on my second collins, so I knew that wasn't going to happen.

Phyllis walked up and sat another Heineken down for David then pulled a card from the box, nosey as could be. It seemed to me that she and Big Earl didn't care much for David, and I didn't understand that.

"Umph..." Phyllis snorted, tossing the card back toward the box. "You got her business cards? What the hell's next, Doc, an office and a secretary?" Phyllis walked off, and David just chuckled and shook his head.

"Amazing," he muttered.

Phyllis and Big Earl called David "Doc" because he was in med school at Vanderbilt, just finishing up his third year. Except for an independent research project, he was about to have a summer off for the first time in three years. He had begun to ask me about my plans for the summer.

You know, as I write this, it occurs to me that while I can't omit David from my college years, I really dread giving you the gory details of my "David time." Those few happy months with him flew by like a glorious blur—crazy times of living feverishly just to be with him, not giving a hoot anymore about my education or anything else. Then came the ugly, horrible fallout—but isn't that typical when something starts that fast and then, God knows, ends even faster? You've heard of someone being left in the dust, an unrecognizable heap left on the side of the road? Well, that was me after the David Eisenberg train hit me.

So, let me get on with this by giving you the crux of it right up front.

I fell sickeningly and irrationally in love with David, a wealthy, Jewish man whose family already had his life mapped out and charted, and that whole master plan did not, believe me, include a little Baptist wench from "Pigtrott, USA"—their term, he said, for all rural areas.

Nonetheless, at age twenty, I happily surrendered my heart, and my virginity, to David Eisenberg during a wonderful Fourth of July visit to the Eisenbergs' summer home in northern Michigan while his parents and sisters were abroad. We flew first class from Nashville to Chicago, where a limo picked us up. That house on Lake Michigan had been built in the 1920s by David's great-grandfather, who had been one of the founders of the Chicago Board of Trade.

So you see, we're talking here about old money and a strong Jewish family that had its own standards and definitions, not to mention its own ideas about marriage and money.

For nearly five months after that trip to Michigan, I floated on air; I went from drinking purple Jesus and tacky vodka collins, to drinking Dom Pérignon and imported top-shelf Dutch vodka straight up on the rocks; I wore Salvatore Ferragamo sandals and eighteen-karat gold earrings, and I quickly learned the difference between drugstore perfume and anything made by Guerlain. So you can see, David was what the kids these days call a "game changer" for me.

That summer, E. A. and I moved into a one-bedroom apartment three blocks off campus, with twin beds and a little kitchenette. It was even closer to the Chi O house than our dorm had been, so she was happy, even though she had to go to summer school, having flunked two of her spring courses. A corner of our little sitting area in the apartment basically became her second closet, which was fine by me, because I was either playing a gig or with David.

And money? Well, let's just say that I easily made enough to pay my part of the rent and utilities, eat enough to get by, and then open a bank account. It seemed every time I played somewhere, another one or two jobs would fall in my lap. Who knows, maybe it was because so much of Nashville was already country music-oriented, but I was walkin' proof that some of the upper- crusts of Music City wanted to hear classical and popular stuff.

I could have gone back to the Hammondses' beach house for a week in August, but a twenty-mule team couldn't have pried me out of Nashville as long as David was there. He said the apartment he shared with two other med students was a pigsty, so the bar at the Hermitage became our place to meet; he kept a running tab with Big Earl, which was always paid on time and with a generous tip.

David took me shopping to replace my plain cotton bras and panties with matching sets in everything from hot pink to lace-trimmed leopard print. My nylon summer pajamas were pushed to the bottom drawer in place of silk and linen nightshirts in beige and French blue. For spending nights between the apartment, the Hermitage, and our weekend getaways, mostly to Memphis, David bought me a really nice leather tote bag to use; it was made of brownish-tan leather with some lettered emblem on it.

"What does that mean?" I asked, genuinely ignorant and pointing at the design.

David looked at me and answered flatly, "Louis Vuitton."

"Who's that?"

We were pulling into the hotel parking lot in his red BMW.

"Never mind," he said, squeezing my boob.

I laughed and slapped at his hand.

"Don't worry about it." He smiled.

Little fool that I was, I didn't.

In early September fall semester started, and E. A. and I decided to stay in the apartment rather than go back to the dorm. By then she was a full-fledged, card-carrying, dyed-in-the-wool Chi Omega of the first order. She had T-shirts, bumper stickers, bathrobes, and assorted jewelry that were all Chi Omega—everything from a diamond lavaliere necklace to a chapter pin and a gold watch. She was as Chi O as anyone could be, I guess, but surprisingly, there was now something else on her mind.

During August at the beach, E. A. had met a young stockbroker from Atlanta, a graduate of Emory University; he was almost thirty years old, single, beautiful, and well-off. His name was Everett Belcher.

"He's one of the Buckhead Belchers," E. A. said.

Apparently being a Buckhead Belcher meant something in Atlanta; I didn't tell E. A. that the only Belchers I'd ever known were some backwood hill folks who brewed rot-gut moonshine and raised hogs.

Anyway, young Mr. Belcher had decided all his dreams and fantasies had become incarnate in the divine Ms. Hammonds—he assured E. A. that he would be in Nashville for every dance, every party, and every football game she wished to attend that fall. And, by golly, he was; it helped, of course, that he had his own airplane. All this caused E. A. to reconsider her plan to hook a Vandy doctor or lawyer.

David began his last year of medical school, explaining to me that he had two of the hardest rotations coming up: surgery and OB/GYN. He said his call schedule for the next few months was going to be unpredictable but that he'd stay in touch with me every day by phone so that we could see each other whenever he had time. He assured me that he'd call regularly, so there was no need for me to try to reach him. That sounded perfectly fine with me. Since the bar at the Hermitage was on his way home, it was still the easiest place for us to meet.

Are you asking yourself yet why I trusted him so much? Why I didn't give any of this a second thought? Well, remember, David was the first man—the first and only man—who had ever shown any real interest in me, who paid any real attention to what I was doing or what I *could* do. If you're thinking about Jimmy Dale, let me just say that no boy from Grantville, Jimmy Dale or anybody else, could have held a candle to David. Even all the Vandy frat boys and the jocks, guzzling their cheap beer and playing grab-ass with each other, seemed silly now compared to David.

David drank imported beer or twelve-year-old scotch. He played the violin. He loved Memphis for its blues clubs and barbeque, and the watch on his wrist was worth more than my momma had ever earned. So you see, nobody I had ever known was even in his league.

I started my junior year by taking the minimum number of hours I could take to keep my scholarship: I took two education courses, one music course, and a PE course. Since school was the last thing on my mind, I wanted the easiest semester I could come up with, and I wanted morning classes so that I could wait by the phone in the afternoons to hear from David. And believe it or not, he did call regularly.

If I told him that E. A. had plans for the evening, he would come by the apartment and we'd drink and make-out, then fall into my twin bed. Then other afternoons he'd call and tell me to meet him at the

Hermitage that evening, where we'd drink, make--out, and fall into one of the upstairs suites. He was always—always-- gone by six in the morning, sometimes even earlier.

"Grace, how many doctors do you know who keep bankers' hours?" he pointed out to me once.

Don't you just cringe when you think about it? I didn't have a phone number for him; I didn't have an address. If I had broken out in red measles or shattered both my legs, I had no idea how to reach him. Later I realized, of course, *that* was exactly how he wanted it.

By then there was only one thing that I enjoyed almost as much as I enjoyed being with David: drinking.

Having now been introduced to truly fine spirits, I developed a taste for vodka on the rocks with a twist of fresh lime that was like heaven to me. Now I not only loved the effects of alcohol, I actually began to love the *taste* of it. Since I no longer attended the frat parties or the pep rallies or even the football games, I had plenty of time to myself, waiting for the phone to ring as I dreamily sipped on my imported nectar supplied by David.

Looking back I later realized that everything began to unravel sometime in early November; I think it was the first week. David called on a Tuesday and told me he'd be at the bar by seven thirty that night. I dropped what I was doing, got dressed, grabbed my bag, and had E. A. drop me off.

I sat there, drinking and talking to Big Earl, until ten forty-five. David never showed- up, and Phyllis, who got off work at eleven, left early and drove me to the apartment.

The next morning, the phone rang at six thirty; David said he was sorry and that he'd gotten tied up.

"Tomorrow night I know for sure I'm free, so I'll see you there," he said.

Thursday night I sat again, this time at our table, and I waited.

And I drank.

On her break, Phyllis came over and sat down, immediately lighting one of her Camels.

"Your doctor--boy stand you up again, kid?" she said. Both she and Earl had begun to rag me about David.

"Don't start, Phyllis...he'll be here," I said, rattling my empty glass gently toward Earl to show I needed another.

Phyllis took a sip of her Coke and a draw from her Camel and glanced around the bar. It wasn't really busy for a Thursday night.

"You know, Grace," she said, "I figured you for a pretty smart girl---being in college and all ---- playing the piano like you do, but, God Almighty, I've decided you're as dumb as a box of hammers."

I glared at her and shook my head dismissively. I was thinking that there was no way she could grasp what was happening with me and David.

My silence didn't deter her one bit.

"So, let's see now...you've been seeing him since what? May?" Phyllis held up her left hand and counted off. "So June, July, August, September, October, and now it's November. Might as well say, what? Five months?" She waved her hand with her fingers spread open.

"Five months, Grace. Think about it. Five months... and where has he taken you? Seems to me all you do is meet him right here in this bar."

She took a draw off her Camel. I just sat, looking at her with as much disinterest as I could muster.

"Damn, girl...don't you ever ask yourself *why*? Why he doesn't take you to nice restaurants...or movies, parties, anywhere? Aren't you the least bit concerned about that?" Phyllis sort of squinted at me.

Big Earl walked over and sloshed my next drink down in front of me, having heard what Phyllis had just said.

"Phyll, leave her alone...you're wastin' your breath," Earl said, turning to walk back to the bar.

I took a drink from the heavy glass tumbler with the Hermitage logo engraved in it. Then I looked up to answer her, working hard to be cool toward her.

"Phyllis...for your information, David *does* take me places. We've been to Memphis about five times now. We go to all the blues clubs there that he likes...we stay at the Peabody...and we eat in all kinds of places." I took another sip.

Phyllis was staring at me.

"And furthermore, if you knew *anything* about doctors or medical school, you'd know that his schedule right now is very hectic, and... there are no doctors with bankers' hours."

Phyllis snickered and looked away then looked back at me.

"Memphis? Are you kiddin' me? *Memphis*? You think he's takin' you to Memphis for the damn barbeque?" Shaking her head, she put out her cigarette, downed the rest of her Coke, and leaned forward.

"Girl, let me tell you somethin'...he's meetin' you right here"—she tapped the tabletop—"and he's takin' you to *Memphis*," she said Memphis very sarcastically, "because somethin' ain't right. Do you hear me? You can write this down, kid...your Mister Doctor ain't squarin' things with you. Somethin' is *up* with this fella...I'm tellin' you that right now."

Suddenly she stood up.

"But you know what? It ain't no skin off old Phyll's nose one way or the other. I just hate to see a nice, young woman get run over by a major-league asshole. My break's over." She walked off.

I had two more drinks and waited until eleven thirty. Then I called E. A. and asked her to come get me.

Waiting across the street from the Hermitage, I stumbled off the curb when she pulled up and I went to get in the Corvette.

E.A. laughed, taking my bag and tossing it behind her seat.

"Good Lord, Grace, you're plastered," she yelled over the radio.

"No, I'm not!" I snapped, slamming the door.

"OK, you're not then." She whipped the 'vette into the street.

I was disappointed. I had a piano gig Friday night at Cumberland Country Club, and David had already said he was working Saturday night, so it would probably be Sunday before I saw him.

E. A. stopped at a red light and looked over at me then turned down the radio.

"I thought you said you've got a test in the morning...in English lit?" she asked.

"Yeah, I do...but I don't care."

Being drunk can make you do and say some stupid, funny-ass things sometimes. I don't have a very clear recollection of what happened next, but E. A. said that at one point she was laughing so hard she nearly ran off the road.

All of a sudden, I reached up and turned off the radio then looked over at E. A. very seriously.

"E. A., are you aware, my dear, that there are leagues of assholes?" I asked.

She glanced over at me.

"Leagues of assholes? You mean...men?" she asked.

According to her, from there I took it and did about a fifteen-minute monologue about *assholes*—minor-league assholes compared to major-league assholes, domestic versus foreign assholes, international authorities that classify assholes, obvious assholes and covert assholes, plus professional versus amateur assholes.

Apparently when we pulled into the parking lot at the apartment, we both fell out of the car, folded over in stitches, and shrieked hysterically all the way up the steps, wiping tears from our eyes. E. A. must have told everybody she knew about that skit, and it never failed to make her laugh all over again, no matter how many times she told it.

I never set my alarm that night, and I slept right through my Friday classes.

A week later, David and I went to Memphis, and I have to say, I couldn't help but think about what Phyllis had said to me, but then he would kiss me or throw his arm around me, and I would forget about it. It was another great weekend.

It wasn't until late Sunday night, on our way back to Nashville, that a cloud floated apprehensively across my mind.

It began when David said that he was going to be very busy during the holidays. On Thanksgiving morning, he explained, he was flying to Chicago, where his family was gathering at his grandparents' house. He said Hanukkah was beginning right after that, and although his family were Reform, they still maintained a rather strict observance of it.

What I knew about Judaism wouldn't have filled a thimble, and David knew that, because he explained that instead of Christmas, they celebrated eights nights of Hanukkah with numerous family gatherings and gifts.

"But, of course, I'll still have to work during all that...so I'll be overloaded," he explained. "That won't be a problem, since you'll be leaving to go home for Christmas, right?"

Honestly, I hadn't given one single thought to the holidays—not Thanksgiving, not Christmas or New Year's. Looking back later on, I asked myself often, just what did I think was going to happen? In my fog-headed, love-sick naïveté did I really believe that he was suddenly going to invite me home with him for the holidays?

As I unpacked my bag that Sunday night, E. A. asked me if I was OK.

"I'm fine," I said, sitting down suddenly on my bed. "In the car tonight, David started talkin' about the holidays. He's spendin' Thanksgiving in Chicago."

She didn't say anything, but I saw her raise her eyebrows—was she a bit surprised or what?

"You know, I've come to dread holidays...I think it's because I hate goin' back to Grantville now. It's just so dull," I said, going back to unpacking.

"So don't go back," E. A. said. "Come to Hammondsville. Everett will be there, and we might end-up going to Atlanta to the Tech game on Saturday. If you come, at least I'll have somebody to ride home with me," she pointed out.

Not go home for Thanksgiving? Just blow off my family? Could I really get by with that?

December 14th. That's the date David's engagement was announced on the front page of the society section of the Sunday *Tennessean Journal*.

E. A. came in from the Chi O Sunday-night meeting looking like someone had killed her dog. I was about to ask her what was wrong, when, without a word, she handed me the tattler section of the Nashville Sunday newspaper.

There was a large, formal photograph of a very serious-looking, attractive young woman named Sharon Deborah Solomon, and the caption read: "Solomon-Eisenberg Engagement."

I sat down on the bed and read the whole thing about thirty times. I didn't cry. I don't think I even said anything. I had already been drinking since finishing my afternoon gig at the Hermitage, so I was buzzed, but the last sentence of the announcement sobered me up as if a bucket of cold water had hit me square in the face: "A May wedding is planned."

A May wedding is planned. A May wedding is planned. Those words began flashing on and off, right behind my eyeballs. At one point I entertained the quick thought that maybe there was another David Jacob Eisenberg who was completing medical school at Vanderbilt in the spring. That delusion didn't last long. Then the black hole opened.

Poor E. A., you had to hand it to her—she stayed right there beside me the rest of the night as I went headfirst into a quart of vodka just as fast as I could. She kept talking to me, but I couldn't tell you anything she said. I fell into a blurry tunnel, where it didn't take long for me to get smashed—I'm talkin' wasted drunk. But I do remember the echo of her voice saying my name.

"Grace...ohhhhh, Grace." E. A. must have said it a hundred times. Then, before I slipped into a semi-unconscious stupor, it became "Grace? Grace? Can you hear me, Grace?"

I didn't want to hear her. I didn't want to hear anything. I didn't want to think or feel. That night was just the beginning.

ᓚᕓ

Lie. Lie, lie, lie, lie, and lie some more. It's amazing how quickly you can get really good at something once you get started. I even enlisted my little brother in my carousel of whoppers. Let me see if I can even list the lies I told, but first let me tell you that I quit everything—*everything*.

I quit going to class. I quit working. I quit eating. I quit showering, and I think the only reason I didn't quit brushing my teeth was because about every other day I couldn't stand the taste in my mouth any longer. But I did not—I could not—quit drinking.

Wayne Tayloe, one of the five boys who lived in the apartment below, had an old pickup, and at some point I talked him into driving me to the bank, where I withdrew every penny I'd saved, $368.58. I made him take me to the liquor store, and I bought a case of cheap vodka and a bag of limes. Back at the apartment, I stuffed the remaining money into an old sock as I half-way wondered how long it would last and what I could use to drink when all of it was gone.

One afternoon, it had to be around the twenty-first of December, E. A. asked me if I needed a ride to the bus station. Wasn't I going home for Christmas? she asked. She was leaving in the morning herself.

No, I was not going home—I was not going anywhere. For a week I'd stumbled between the sofa, my bed, and the kitchen, and I did not intend to change that routine. I told E. A. not to worry about me.

"Have a very Merry Christmas...and cheers," I said, downing the drink I was holding. She stood there gazing at me with a worried look in her eyes, but I just walked away.

After E. A. left the next morning, I called home, collect, and told Aunt Doris that I had so many holiday parties lined-up to play for I just couldn't get away. Not going home for Thanksgiving was one thing, but now not coming home for Christmas was another, so I expanded my lie: I told my aunt that I'd been hired to play at a huge Christmas Eve pageant downtown, because their original pianist had broken her wrist and that it was a big deal and the money was great—lie, lie, lie.

Then I told her some other people in the apartment complex were staying and that we'd planned a big pot-luck Christmas dinner and that I'd be fine: lie, lie. Aunt Doris bought it, but she said Momma would have a fit—which she did.

I had failed to show-up for all of my finals, so I took incompletes for the whole fall semester. I completely trashed my reputation as PIANO GRACE; I ignored the remainder of the holiday gigs I had booked for

December, plus my commitment at the Hermitage. I just stood them all up—didn't call, didn't explain, just didn't show-up.

During those first couple of weeks, I did some really weird, creepy, sometimes-funny things, the details of which I mostly don't remember. Apparently Wayne witnessed some of them.

For instance one night, I think it might have even been Christmas night, I took my box of business cards out to the parking lot, down by the Dumpster, and set them on fire. I stood there, barefoot in my dirty pajamas, and watched them burn. A familiar bitter echo rose with the dark smoke and drifted in the cold air around me: *who did I think I was anyway?*

Then I walked back inside and dug through the trash until I found that newspaper section. With drunken exactness, I meticulously cut-out the engagement announcement, smoothed it out carefully, and taped it to the front of the refrigerator. After that, I would stand and stare at it.

"Sharon Deborah Solomon is an honor graduate of Bryn Mawr College in Philadelphia, where she was president of Bryn Mawr College Democrats and a member of the Social Justice Club. Miss Solomon recently returned from an extended visit in Israel and has been accepted to the political science masters program at the University of Chicago, where next summer Mr. Eisenberg will begin his residency in internal medicine. A May wedding is planned."

I had a twisted need to wallow in the hard truth, in the piercing, breathtaking details of the whole thing. Every time I read it, another of David's vague, practical-sounding explanations to me would fall into place.

Another afternoon, about half-way through a quart of Smirnoff, I put on some things David had given me—hot pink underwear, a silk nightshirt, my Ferragamo sandals, French perfume, gold earrings, and the latest gem, a silk Hermes scarf.

I sat on the sofa, watching *Hollywood Squares*, drinking, and letting the phone ring off the hook. I had made the decision, determinedly, that I did not want to talk to *anybody*—and besides, something told me that it was *not* David on the end of the line--- that it would never be David again.

The only thing David had ever written to me was a card enclosed with the red scarf, the exact same shade of red as his car, which arrived at the apartment just after Thanksgiving—the gift he sent me directly from Marshall Field in Chicago. The card said that he was staying in Chicago after the holidays for a six-week seminar, that he hoped I had a Merry Christmas, and that he would *"see me later."* He signed it with a big, bold *D*.

Now I taped that card on the refrigerator door, beside the newspaper clipping, so that I could stare at them alternately. One night, thick-tongued, cross-eyed drunk, I yelled down the steps for Wayne to come-up.

"I want your opinion on something, Waynie," I bellowed from the front door.

I showed him the card and asked him to speculate on the male definition of *later*. Could it not, I wagered, mean later as in another lifetime altogether? I started laughing hysterically at the look on his face as he just stood there, probably pretty disgusted at what he saw.

Wayne tried to get me to eat something. I refused. He told me then to go to bed, and he locked the door on his way out.

Let me tell you here a little something about Wayne, most of which I didn't even know myself until later.

If it was possible to be even more redneck and countrified than I was, Gary Wayne Tayloe was. From a large farming family in south Alabama, Wayne was a twenty-four-year-old combat veteran, having done two tours in Vietnam with the First Marine Division. Wayne was determined to get a college degree from Vanderbilt with his GI benefits. He and his younger brother, plus two younger cousins and another guy, all shared the two-bedroom apartment directly beneath E. A. and me.

Two of the guys worked construction; one was on a baseball scholarship, and the other one was a senior with hopes of starting graduate school.

Throughout that whole apartment complex, Wayne Tayloe was the closest thing there was to a real-live adult; he was the voice of reason, and later on I realized why E. A. thought the world of him.

"Thank God Wayne was there," E. A. said more than once. That was Wayne: a good, strong, country boy, who had done his duty without complaint. Although I didn't realize it then----much less have enough sense to appreciate it----Wayne was a rock.

꒰ꕤ꒱

One morning, in a rush of hung-over clarity, I realized that the one thing that would tip-off my family about the black hole that had swallowed me whole on December 14th was Vanderbilt University, specifically the Music Department and the registrar's office. How in the name of Sam Hill was I going to keep them—my family—out of my wrecked life, out of my sad personal business? A quick solution made its way into my throbbing, foggy head—Wesley.

There was now a phone at Momma's so I called there, hoping Wesley hadn't left yet for school. Sure enough, he answered. Momma had already gone to work.

"Grace? It's a good thing you called...Momma is pissed- off big-time at you," he said immediately, sounding almost pleased.

"Why...because I didn't come for Christmas?"

"Yep... she said college scholarship or not, people are supposed to be *at home* at Christmas. So why didn't you come?" he chirped.

"Wesley, I don't want to go into it...I just need you to do something for me and to keep your mouth shut about it. I'll pay you forty dollars," I said.

"Forty bucks? Really?"

"Yes, really. Will you do it?"

"Yeah...what is it?"

I bribed my little brother into intercepting every piece of mail from Vanderbilt University to Momma's address and to Grammie's house. Yes, I know—it's a federal crime, but I didn't think about that, and I wouldn't have cared anyway. All I wanted was for them not to get any mail that would cause me to have to explain *anything*. Just how long I thought this plan would work didn't cross my mind right then. All I knew was that for forty dollars the problem was solved for the time being.

"What's wrong, Grace? Are you flunkin' out?"

"Nooo...I'm not flunkin' out, Wesley...just do it, and tell Momma that I'll call her Sunday night," I said.

"She's been tryin' to call you... she said if she didn't hear from you soon she was drivin' to Nashville to find your young ass."

"Well, tell her that I called... but whatever you do *don't* tell her about our deal...about the mail." My mind was racing, lie, lie, lie. "You hear me? And just tell her that somethin's wrong with the phone in my apartment...that it's been out of order, but that I'm fine. OK?"

"Yeah, OK, Grace. What do you want me to do with the mail when I get it?"

The answer popped right into my head.

"Take it down to the incinerator...you know, down by the back gate at the mill?"

"Oh yeah...neat-o. I can do that. You know, Grace, your Christmas presents are still in there on your bed; there's one from Miss Bertie."

"OK...I'll get them later. Bye, Wes, and remember—don't tell anybody about the mail. I'll send you the money in a pink-striped envelope... look for it." I could use some of E. A.'s personal stationery.

"OK...thanks, Grace...bye."

I hung up.

I wish I could tell you that I felt bad or guilty or ashamed of what I was doing, but I didn't. As long as I kept enough vodka in me, I didn't have to feel anything. So far, so good.

Sometime after Christmas, but before the thirty-first—the mailman delivered a package to me from Hammondsville. Inside was a Christmas present from E. A., a sterling-silver picture frame with a picture of me and E. A. that Everett had taken at the Georgia-Georgia Tech football game Thanksgiving weekend. It was a really good picture of the two of us, and on the back, E. A. had written the date and "To Grace with love, Merry Christmas."

I stared at myself and knew that that photograph was the last one taken of me before everything went to hell, before my life—and my heart—split right smack-ass into two sad sections: before David, after David. I looked good in that picture, like I was sane and normal and pretty happy. It was a really good picture of E. A....and a fool.

With the picture was a note from E. A., saying that even though I wasn't a Chi O, I was the one that was most truly her "sister." Then she wished me a Merry Christmas and said that something must be wrong with the phone, because she'd been trying to call.

E. A. said she'd be back on January 2.

I looked around that apartment. She'll die when she sees this place, I thought, but too damn bad. E. A.'s world was safe and sound, and nothing would ever really threaten it—if she had a fit, she'd get over it. Besides, I knew her life would always be one home run after another anyway.

E.A.'s twenty-inch portable television in the living room stayed on day and night, on the same channel. Seemed like every time I turned around *Hollywood Squares* was on, but who knows, since time had become irrelevant to me.

There were some empty pizza boxes on the kitchen counter, courtesy of Wayne, and the trash in the corner was headed up the wall— empty cereal boxes, cracker boxes, peanut-butter and cheese-spread jars, and, of course, vodka bottles overflowed the container, but I just kept stacking. I didn't really remember it, but evidently I had eaten what little food had been in the kitchen, plus whatever Wayne offered me sometimes.

Although I hadn't gotten dressed in over ten days, most of my clothes were strewn all over the bedroom and bathroom—don't ask me why. At some point I had rifled through a box of my music, because that, too, was scattered everywhere. The place was a wreck, but I couldn't care less.

Meanwhile, E. A. had celebrated her twenty-first birthday on December 30 and with Mr. Hammonds's blessing, Everett Belcher placed a two-carat diamond on her left hand. She said yes, yes, yes, and they spent New Year's Eve dancing the night away at Atlanta's Piedmont Driving Club. A picture of them appeared in the *Atlanta Journal*; E. A. was wearing a designer gown in teal silk as she gazed up at Everett, who looked boldly into the camera. Like I said, one home run after another.

"Grace... this has *got* to stop."

E.A. was standing in front of me with her hands on her hips, blocking *Hollywood Squares*, which was blaring from the television. She had been back nearly two days, during which she had cleaned and scrubbed and taken out garbage and stripped the beds and done the laundry—while I sat keeping company with Mr. Smirnoff or slept, semi-comatose, on the sofa. In fairness, it was past time for a conniption fit; she'd earned it.

I rattled the ice in my glass and just looked at her.

"Damn it, Grace...I *mean* it. It's GOT to stop—now," she said in an angry tone.

I tried to lean around her to see Louie Nye in the bottom left square.

"I want you to get up, go in there and take a shower, and get yourself dressed. Do your hair and makeup, pull yourself together, and start acting like you've got some sense. You've got to go register for your classes—tomorrow is the last day."

She reached and turned off the TV, so I gave up leaning, dug the vodka-soaked lime slice out of the bottom of my glass—my new favorite snack—and bit into it. Then, doing my best to focus, I looked up at her again.

She continued in a softer tone, "Ohhhhh, Grace...you *can't* go on like this. You really can't...have you looked at yourself? Have you looked in a mirror? This is ridiculous...why, you..."

The rant continued, but I'm not sure for how long. I zoned out.

Then an innocent gesture, a little meaningless habit of E. A. Hammonds's, penetrated my impaired, pickled brain. E. A. raised her left hand to push back her bangs, and when she did, her big diamond engagement ring flashed impressively. It took only a split second, but it was at that very moment in time that my momma—good ol' Arlene—whose crass influence I had assumed was buried under Grammie's Bible teachings, Chopin concertos, and Miss Bertie's petit fours emerged from the depths of my inveterate psyche.

Without so much as a hesitation or a pause, I said something that I had never said to anybody, something I'd never even *dreamed* I'd ever say to anybody. It was behavior so far removed from who I was, and who I ever thought I'd be, that it would have made more sense if a second nose had popped-out of my forehead or if I'd looked down and found two giant duck feet where mine had just been. The words flowed right-out of my mouth, rolled off my tongue so effortlessly that you'd think I was saying my own middle name. The tone, the cadence—all of it—was classic Arlene Stevens. I plunked that half-chewed lime slice back into my empty glass and looked my best friend straight in the face.

"Kiss my ass, E. A."

⌒つ

So that's how it went—for I'm not sure how long.

I didn't register for classes, and one day fat Janelle, from Dr. Heller's office, called the apartment. E. A. answered and tried to get me to take the phone. I refused, but while E. A. held out the receiver, I yelled from across the room, "I quit, Janelle...do you hear me? I quit...I'm not comin' back to school. This is Grace Stevens, and as of right now, I'm with-drawin' from Vanderbilt University."

Mr. Gaines called from the Hermitage, and E. A. told him I was sick and that she'd have me call him back soon.

"Why'd you do that, E. A.? I'm *not* gonna call him," I mumbled at her.

She was unloading groceries again. There was now enough food in that little kitchenette to feed a high-school football team.

"And why the hell do you keep haulin' all this stuff in here? I'm not hungry...and there's no way you can eat all of it." I plopped down on the sofa.

E. A. went right-on with what she was doing.

"Well, you never know...you might suddenly decide to clean- up and have some scrambled eggs and toast. Who knows..." she said, trying to sound hopeful.

By then E. A. and Wayne had managed to get me to shower and wash my hair, but I was still wearing the same clothes for four and five days at a stretch. My nails were ragged and ugly; my skin was blotchy and broken- out, but I didn't care. Next to drinking, my favorite thing had become sleeping. For someone who had always been a light sleeper, I could now sleep through anything. Maybe it was because I didn't care about anything. There was nothing that mattered to me, so if the whole city went up in flames, I would have just slept through it. It was a great, dependable escape—once I got drunk enough, I now would make my way over to my bed and crash there, sometimes for over twenty-four hours. Wayne told E. A. he had never seen anybody sleep so much.

Staying drunk or at least well under the influence most of the time had its perks—the ordinary details of life passed right by me, so it did not occur to me that there was still my share of the rent and utilities to pay. I didn't even think about it, and E. A. had gotten to where she wouldn't have asked me for the time of day, much less for money. She was paying for everything.

Wayne would no longer drive me to the liquor store, but I found some guy living behind us in a house, and he'd bring me two half-gallons at a time for a five-dollar tip. Door-to-door delivery of Smirnoff, Popov, Gilbeys—it didn't matter; I'd drink whatever was cheapest.

I no longer had to step-out the front door for any reason, and it was just as well, since I looked like an escapee from a refugee camp. Thin, unkempt, red-eyed, stringy-haired, and sullen, I was about as ugly a slob as you'd find anywhere, but I didn't care—not one whit.

⌒〜〇

Sometime in early February, E. A. walked in with a long dress bag—obviously another major purchase. As usual, I was drunk, but now something else was beginning to brew and bubble inside me. I later realized that, in many ways, that demon was inherent—I came by it honestly, but even so, that didn't make it any less ugly.

You know, it's always been said that there are two kinds of drunks. There are the drunks who get happy and tell jokes and sit down over in the corner, not bothering anybody, and drink till they pass out.

Then there's the other kind—the drunks who get more and more smart-mouthed with every drink. These drunks gradually become so belligerent and obnoxious that there's nothing else left for them to do but just get mad. These are the mean, angry drunks who often start something that someone else finishes for them.

Well, being a simple, quiet drunk for a while had suited me, I guess, but now I was evolving—I was getting sarcastic and nasty. And remember, I had yet to shed a single tear over any of this. I never cried, and I never whined or moaned about what had happened —never.

So E. A. walked in one afternoon with a long, white dress bag, and I said—actually more like bellowed—sarcastically, "Well, let me guess... the divine Miss Hammonds has picked- out her wedding dress, right? So let's have a look..." And with one mean and extremely accurate snatch, I ripped the bag half-way off the dress and the dress off the fancy, white hanger, and the whole thing right out of E. A.'s grasp. The dress fell to the floor. It was *not* a wedding dress. It was her new red velvet gown to wear to the SAE's Valentine dance that Everett was taking her to.

E. A. froze, her eyes wide with shock and hurt. She didn't speak or move, and at first neither did I. Then she looked at me, probably thinking that surely I'd apologize and immediately pick it up, but I didn't. Instead, I busted-out laughing as I stumbled toward the bedroom, yelling back over my shoulder, "Just what we need around here...another damn *dress*..."

E. A. turned slowly and picked- up her purse and keys. Good ol' Wayne, carrying in E. A.'s dry cleaning and a case of Diet Rite for her, had stopped in the doorway and seen the whole thing.

E. A. walked by him on her way out the door, leaving the pile of red velvet right there on the floor. I couldn't tell you where she went or how long she was gone. Wayne must have picked-up the dress; the next morning it was back on the hanger and hanging from the kitchen doorframe. There was no sign of E. A.

Conveniently—and more, sadly—I don't remember this incident, but hearing about it later, the first thing I asked myself was why E. A. didn't pack- up and move out. Wouldn't you? I know I would have. But E. A. didn't move out. She *did* begin to keep her distance from me, but she went right on cleaning- up, bringing in groceries, paying the bills, going to class, and fine-tuning her wardrobe. Her wedding was set for the first Saturday in September.

When she asked me to be her maid of honor, I just glared at her. Me... at her wedding...standing up there at the altar in some frilly, sweetheart-saccharine dress, trying to look like I had good sense? Yeah right, E. A., I thought as I opened another half- gallon of vodka, me—*your maid of honor*. What a joke.

She told me later that she just kept believing that I'd snap out of it—that I'd suddenly see that there was nothing to do but go on with my life and meet someone else, someone better, someone who really loved me. (Someone better than David? Sure, that was gonna happen, I'd tell myself.)

At some point, I remember her telling me to stop taking it all out on myself and that I was mad at the wrong person.

"Grace, *he's* the problem, not you. He used you, and he's a low-down, sorry *bastard*. Why don't you get mad at *him*, for God's sake?" E.A. said one night.

There's no telling what I said back to her, but I know exactly what I was thinking: get mad at David? For what? For giving me the most wonderful five months of my dull, stupid, hillbilly life? That wasn't going to happen—ever.

Good, little Baptist girl that I was, I knew that now I was ruined. De-flowered, tainted, no longer virtuous and pure, I was clearly a slattern.

And on top of being a fallen woman, I was also an idiot—a gullible, little fool who had given myself, wholly and willingly, to a man who had never once said –never so much as uttered--the word "love" to me. Every time that thought crossed my mind, I drank with renewed vigor. *Fool* now alternated with the steady flashing of *"...a May wedding is planned,"* just behind my eyeballs, but enough Smirnoff could—by God—stop that infernal flashing.

I can tell you this about drinking—no matter if you do your dead-level, bull's-eye *best* to drown yourself in booze, to climb right smack into one bottle after another, the world outside goes right on with its business. Telephone calls, mail delivery, birthdays, holidays, doctor appointments, and flat tires, they all go on pretty much as usual. The boozer doesn't know, or care, but it all goes right on, one day after another. I say this because while I stumbled around in my bombed-out black hole—my own personal, hellish vacuum, you could say—letters from home piled- up, left unopened, but things were happening.

Wayne started driving by the Hermitage in his old truck, looking for a red BMW; he had a flat tire one night and nearly got hit by a bus fixing it. No one ever asked, and Wayne never said, exactly what he intended to do if he had *found* the red BMW.

A box arrived from Grantville for me-- a new jumper from Aunt Doris, brownies from Grammie, and a ten-dollar bill from Momma. Wesley had his fifteenth birthday and got his driver's permit, and Miss Bertie went to a new doctor in Atlanta.

So while life went on, winter fumbling its way toward spring, I had my first alcoholic hallucination, which didn't bother me too much, but it scared E. A. shitless- crazy. She said at first she thought I was dreaming but soon realized that I was, indeed, wide-awake... just completely out of it.

Apparently I had about a ten-minute conversation with—of all people—my daddy, during which I asked him numerous questions, demanded answers, recalled specific incidents-- both sad and funny-- and then told him to leave, to "just get the hell out." A few minutes later, I answered the phone, which was actually ringing, and told "him" not to call here again. Then I jerked the phone out of the wall and—evidently with considerable strength and accuracy—threw it through the apartment's wide front window. Whoever the actual caller was, can you just imagine what they must have thought?

E. A. ran out the door to get Wayne, but at the sound of the window shattering, he had already jumped- up from the Thursday night poker game and was racing out the door toward the steps.

"Wayne, she's gone crazy!" E. A. cried as he raced past her up the steps.

Rushing through the doorway, he took one look at me—by then slumped on the sofa—before manhandling me into the bathroom, where he held me up over the toilet, poking his finger down my throat until I puked and puked, then finally quietly passed out.

As E. A., shaking and crying, wiped my face, he checked my pulse, then looked at her and said flatly, "We gotta do something—she's killin' herself."

14

Grammie knew something was wrong. Don't ask me how she knew, but she knew. To Wesley's credit—if you want to call it that—he kept our deal; even when Grammie cornered him one afternoon, he didn't tell her anything, but still, Grammie knew. So what did she do without saying a word to anybody? She got dressed one morning and walked up the hill to Bertie El's big house.

Talk about wanting to be a fly on the wall somewhere...I have always wondered how that little tête-à-tête went, but I never heard any of the details. I do know that Miss Bertie was also very upset that I hadn't come home for Christmas and that she agreed with Grammie that something was certainly amiss.

I also know now that Grammie didn't get out the door and down the driveway before Bertie El Hewitt had her old friend, Dr. Aaron Heller, head of Vanderbilt University's Music Department, on the phone. Yep, you heard me right—Miss Bertie had known Dr. H for many, many, years, but she had never let on to it. Did she have a hand in getting me that scholarship in the first place? Had she been using her connections and influence to make sure I got the opportunity of a lifetime? I'll never know for sure, but hey, wouldn't you say it'd be a pretty safe bet?

It's really not important for you to hear the exact sequence of events that unfolded that week after the telephone went through the window—and it's a good thing it's not important, because I really don't know everything that happened. I was too busy taking a wrecking ball to my whole life.

It doesn't take long to lose a lot of things once you decide that nothing matters to you. In a little over ninety days, I'd lost more than you might imagine...starting right off the bat with my piano skills.

I didn't touch a keyboard for I don't know how long...it was nearly six whole months, I think. Oh, I didn't actually forget how to read music, but because of the thick fog encasing my brain, my hands and fingers lost a lot of the memory that I'd built up in them for years and years. Later on, when I finally did go back to it, recovering my accuracy and technique was not easy; I could identify everything on a page of music in front of me, but there was a long, fuzzy delay between my head and my hands. The doctors said that brain cells don't regenerate, and I had slaughtered several million of mine with alcohol. It would take time.

Another thing I lost was my scholarship, and my class standing within the music majors in my year group at Vanderbilt. And—I lost my driver's license.

I had always been a very good driver. Momma and Jimmy Dale had taught me to drive, and I was a safe, cautious driver. I had driven Momma's Corvair and Aunt Doris's car, and once or twice, I had driven E. A.'s Corvette, just from one side of Nashville to campus. I'd never had so much as a parking ticket, but I wasn't all that impressed with that fact, since I knew I was years and years away from ever having a car of my own anyway.

But unfortunately, what reason and judgment I'd ever had about driving were something else I lost in the bottom of a vodka bottle that spring.

At some point—I'm told—I threatened E. A. with a genuine ass kickin' when she tried to tell me one night that she was worried about me and was gonna call my family. I'm not sure whether this was before or after the telephone went through the front window, but regardless of that, she must have believed my threats. She didn't call my family.

Instead, she went to the Music Department and talked to Janelle... gave her the whole sad tale, evidently from start to finish.

Janelle told everything to Dr. Heller, who was very concerned about me and who happened to know the Eisenbergs, and of their brilliant, handsome son, David. Then, of course, that started a whole other ball rolling-- or I should say, a whole new grapevine for information exchange that eventually became your standard shit-storm.

The scariest thing about alcoholic blackouts is that you not only don't remember what you did or said...you don't remember even being on the planet. You can lose hours, even whole days, and that means you are in no position to even deny anything. You can't say, "Oh, that wasn't me; I was at home in bed by then." You can't say that, because you don't even know what day it is, much less where you were at any given time. You're gone—checked- out-- in an alcohol-induced absence. I know....because I've been there.

Late on a Saturday night in early April, I got the keys to E. A.'s car, and, wearing nothing but some cutoff blue jeans and a red University of Georgia sweat shirt, I went for an extended drive on Interstate 40—*in the wrong direction*. You heard me—I went west, toward Memphis, into eastbound traffic.

I drove that Corvette up an exit ramp and pulled head-on into traffic, just as if I had good sense---and I did it in a driving rainstorm, with the parking brake on, smoking and grinding the whole time. Thanks to all the swerving and braking and sliding, and greater thanks to God Almighty, I didn't kill anybody, and I didn't completely total E. A.'s white Corvette. Some quick-thinking truckers, communicating on their CB radios, and an off-duty Tennessee state trooper stopped the eastbound traffic, while the Corvette was forced into a side guardrail, bringing it to a nasty halt.

Although I wasn't injured, I suddenly passed right out—blotto, lights-out—right there at the scene, so an ambulance came and transported me to Methodist hospital, where for almost thirty-six hours, I was a Jane Doe.

The only information they had was E. A.'s name from the car's glove box, and with it there was no working phone number and only a

Hammondsville, Georgia, post-office box. No one knew who I was or where I lived—they only knew that I was in acute respiratory failure from alcohol poisoning. And lucky me, I don't remember a thing.

In the meantime, Mr. and Mrs. Hammonds got scared out of their wits when the Tennessee Highway Patrol and DMV called at four o'clock Sunday morning; they assumed E. A. had been in a wreck and began trying to call the apartment, but there was no working phone. Next they called the Chi O house, and one of E. A.'s sorority sisters was sent immediately to find her, which took several hours, because by then E. A. and Wayne were out in his old truck, looking for me.

Later that Sunday, Cooper drove Miss Bertie--- completely unaware of all this-- to Nashville, where she was having dinner at the Hellers' that evening. Her plan was to surprise me on Monday morning and then go with me to meet with Dr. H. to hopefully salvage my scholarship. But trust me, Miss Bertie was the one who ended- up surprised—or more like shocked.

At seven thirty Monday morning, Janelle appeared at Dr. Heller's back door; she had received a panicked phone call from E. A. Hammonds about Grace Stevens.

And lastly, based on details pieced together from Janelle and Bertie El about Grace and one David Eisenberg, Mr. and Mrs. Heller intended to have a long, private chat with their old friends, the Eisenbergs, about their son's recent little fling that had jeopardized the future of an unsophisticated, but talented, Vanderbilt scholarship student. I guess in some Jewish families no son is ever beyond answering to his parents.

All this was happening while Jane Doe's blood was drawn; her stomach was pumped not just once, but twice. IV fluids were administered; vitals were monitored hourly; a full range of skull X- rays were completed, and law enforcement and hospital social workers attempted to identify her.

Then, by late morning on Monday, the pieces fell into place, and the mystery was solved: according to several different people, Jane Doe was Grace Stevens, a Vanderbilt co-ed.

c◯

Around two thirty on Monday afternoon, I woke up. There were three people in my hospital room—three sets of eyes trained directly on me. There were no smiles, no happy greetings of relief or understanding.

No one said a word. E.A. was standing near the window; fat Janelle was sitting in a chair at the foot of the bed, and Miss Bertie was standing beside the bed, on my left. I wish I had the words to describe the three distinct looks on their faces, but I don't.

I'll just tell you that E. A. had been crying and looked very scared. Janelle looked as mad as an old, sore-tailed cat, and Miss Bertie...well, the best word for her is just plain sad. That look, that gaze of being so utterly let down, so completely disappointed and stabbed- in- the- gut, really broke my heart. It broke my heart in a whole different way from what David Eisenberg had done. Minutes passed as still no words were spoken.

Maybe all the tears I had never cried were backed-up, waiting for an opening—I don't know-- but a dam broke, either in my head or my heart, and suddenly floods and geysers of tears poured from my eyes. I sobbed—ashamed, embarrassed, and just plain sick—for a very long time. E. A. brought over a box of hospital tissues and handed them to me one at a time, until she started to cry, too. Miss Bertie motioned for her to leave, and she did, nudging Janelle to go out with her.

So there we were—Miss Bertie and I left alone, me sniveling and wiping, she looking with painful resolve at me. Finally I got enough control of myself to actually speak in a hoarse, broken whisper. "Please...please, Miss Bertie, don't tell them...don't tell Momma and Aunt Doris...please don't tell Grammie...please, please... just don't tell them," I pleaded, gasping between sobs and trying not to choke to death or puke right there on the spot.

Without a word, Miss Bertie slowly dragged the chair from the foot of the bed around to the side, and then she sat down, settling herself, it looked to me, for a long spell, if need be. I knew then that she would sit there for as long as it took. Smoothing her skirt as she crossed her legs, she looked me dead straight in the face and finally spoke.

"Oh, don't worry, Grace...I'm not going to tell them a thing..." she said calmly.

Our eyes locked, and I realized then that her sentence wasn't finished.

"...you are."

∽⟲

If someone asked you to draw or paint or generally describe anger, what would you come up with? There's the raging bull and the snarling dog and the stormy sea; there's shattered glass and white-hot screams and baseball bats flung in the air and hair-on-fire conniption fits. Right? I ask this because after my first week at Mountain Creek Hospital and Rehab Center, that's what my therapist said to me.

"Grace, what does your anger look like to you?"

You've heard of people snapping? Well, that's what happened to me in that hospital room in Nashville with Miss Bertie. As if there wasn't already enough serious, undeniable proof that I needed help, I went ahead and sealed the deal once and for all by finally going truly nuts-o berserk.

Ten days later, I couldn't really tell the therapist what the anger *looked* like, but I knew what I felt when Miss Bertie told me that I— good-girl Grace—was going to have to tell my family. Something akin to a giant, black python crawled out of my gut, wrapped itself around my windpipe in a choke hold, and made me want to kill somebody— anybody. It just so happened that poor Miss Bertie was closest at the time...but luckily so were several nurses and orderlies.

Two thousand, four hundred and five dollars, that's what it cost for eight weeks at Mountain Creek to get me out of the black hole that had evidently been slowly opening around me for many years and into which I had finally fallen after David. Miss Bertie wrote the check and never so much as batted an eye. And, yes, I did tell my family *everything* in a long, pathetic letter that took me three days to write.

Visitors to Mountain Creek were "strongly discouraged" until a patient had completed the fourth week of the program, so thank God, by the time Momma and Aunt Doris and Grammie actually saw me, I was in much better shape. Miss Bertie had spared them from seeing the worst. No doubt I looked different—hell, I *was* different—but by the time I walked into the visitors' lounge that Saturday morning at least I was recognizable to them.

Birthday cake, balloons, presents, they brought it all. And tell the truth now, how many people do you know who've had their twenty-first birthday in rehab?

The trouble with shrinks and counselors and therapists and all that talking and sharing they do with you is that it really hurts—before it really helps. At first I hated it...I hated it because I was full of anger and resentment and fear, all of which I had drowned for the last five months with vodka and lime juice. In the process, I had damaged my liver, wrecked my looks, and pretty much torpedoed my young life in every way imaginable.

How the hell would talking and whining about it to some hand-holding, middle-aged, grandmotherly counselor in a clinic office help that? Well, it took two sessions every day for three weeks before something shifted in me, and it *did* begin to help.

Rather than inundate you with details, I will sum it up as quickly as I can. With the grandmother/counselor, I "dealt"—her word for analyzing and learning from an issue—with David, which led me backward to my daddy, which brought me to Momma and my family; then I dealt with my musical talent, which brought me forward to success and rewards but also pressure and stress. Then we got to college, with its ups, downs, and "new opportunities"—her words—and then to peer acceptance and alcohol abuse, which brought up family again. Then we went on to love, sex, self-worth, and—back to David.

That was one helluva roller-coaster ride I took in that little corner office, I tell you. It was enough to often make me sick to my stomach; I cussed, cried, raged, laughed, sulked, denied, confessed, and struggled with truths and facts as well as myths and fantasies. It was *not* fun.

I left there sometimes feeling so low the ants knew me by my first name. I'm talkin' low-down, more discouraged and disgusted than I ever imagined I could be. Close-up and personally, I wrestled and finally grasped the spiked horns of my depression, and according to the counselor, *that* signaled progress.

While we all have our baggage and our demons and our own lessons to learn, *nobody* goes through intense treatment and comes out the other side of it without at least gaining a few insights about themselves. It's impossible not to. I mean, you sit for hours, recounting memories and figuring out why you thought this or felt that or why you did something or didn't do it—it's a trip into who you really are, believe me.

In hindsight, I can tell you that it was all worth it...I just wouldn't want to make a habit of it.

I came to see and understand a lot about myself and my family, and I'm happy to say that it changed me, all for the better. So there were gains for all the pain.

Two days before I was discharged from Mountain Creek, Wayne and E. A. drove up to see me. The Corvette had been repaired and looked brand-new, and Wayne was thrilled to be behind the wheel, even if the price for that was having to listen to E. A. talk non-stop the whole time.

E. A. was going to stay in our little apartment through the summer and take two more courses before leaving in August to go home for the wedding. Once she and Everett were settled in Atlanta, she was going back to school at Emory to finish her degree.

When she and Wayne came to visit, she brought five *Bride* magazines with her and showed me her top three picks for her dress and several ideas for the bridesmaids. And, yes, I agreed to be her maid of honor.

Good ol' Wayne, his GI Bill benefits had finally been set-up, and he was starting at Vanderbilt in the summer session. The south Alabama farm boy, the marine combat veteran, was going to study American literature. That day he hugged me long and hard and said that I looked a helluva lot better than I'd looked the last time he'd seen me—I wasn't sure when that had been, and I really didn't want to know.

I looked in Wayne's eyes, and I saw something strong and kind in him...something that even war had not dampened. I realized that I would probably never know everything he had done for me and that in him, E. A. and I had—by simple, dumb luck—found a genuinely good man and a good friend. Grateful and embarrassed by what I figured he had seen and done for me, I thanked him and asked him to stay in touch. He said he would see me at E. A.'s wedding and he wanted at least one dance with me.

On a bright spring Friday afternoon in late May, Momma and Aunt Doris arrived at Mountain Creek to take me home. I left with two different medications that I was to take for the next six months, and a referral to a clinic in Knoxville for a monthly follow-up appointment.

An hour before my discharge, I met with my therapist and two different doctors around a table in the boardroom. They told me that if I wanted to live—and especially if I wanted to live a healthy, productive life—I could never again drink alcohol. With their numbers and charts, they showed me what I had done to my liver and pancreas, and then I heard how the EMT in the ambulance on I-40 had saved my life, because I had basically quit breathing.

"Grace, honey, you have been to the brink...now you have a second chance. Make the most of it...and remember, living takes more than just talent. Honestly, I hope I never see you again," my grandma-therapist said, smiling at me.

When I walked out of that hospital, all the innumerable shades of spring greens glowed, from the grass right at my feet all the way through every shimmering new leaf and bud. The bright sun blinded me momentarily as its glorious warmth spread over me. It felt so good I nearly gasped; I actually paused, closed my eyes, and stood still to soak it all in. My God, I thought, I feel like I've survived some kind of horrible accident. And in a way, I certainly had.

The very next evening, David married Sharon Solomon.

How is it possible to grow- up in a town and know its streets and build-ings and neighborhoods as well as you know your own name but not really see—or appreciate-- so many details? That's how I felt sitting in the backseat of Aunt Doris's car as we drove through Grantville late that afternoon.

I suddenly saw things for the first time that had obviously been right under my nose all my life: two huge magnolia trees by the entrance to the State Bank building, rows and rows of blooming quince along the grade-school playground, the ancient rock wall where the first court-house once stood. Those things had always been there, but I guess chil-dren just don't notice. I was no longer a child.

There is no doubt in my mind that most of Grantville knew about what had happened. I'm sure there were several juicy, gossipy versions floating around, but not one person ever mentioned it to me. Everybody—*everybody*-- I saw was kind and glad to see me. Mrs. Bell at the Kress store told me to let her know when I'd like to start working; she needed some part-time help for the summer. And at the diner, Mrs. Thakakis insisted on making a special batch of pimento cheese just for me.

Momma had really fixed-up our garage apartment. The twin beds had new bedspreads, and there were matching curtains and cute throw rugs. Wesley was moved back to the sleeper sofa, which was fine with him, since Momma had bought a small, color television that was the answer to his prayers. I couldn't believe how much he had grown in a year; he was an excellent baseball player, already co-captain of the high-school team.

Things at Aunt Doris and Grammie's house were still the same. The cover had been kept closed on my piano, but it had been tuned in prepa-ration for my arrival. Everything was exactly as I had left it—my stacks of music, my muse statue, and, of course, all the pictures.

When I finally sat down at the piano one afternoon, thinking I was alone, I attempted to play "Turkish March." I couldn't do it; it was gone. I stumbled and fumbled, my hands and fingers stiff and clumsy as if they had basically never played before. I think it was then that the full weight of what I had lost finally struck me. Here was a piece of music that I had been able to play practically blindfolded, and now it was gone, gone from my brain, gone from my fingers. Gently, I closed the piano lid and covered my face with my hands.

"Bertie El says it will all come back, Grace." Grammie was standing in the doorway, holding a grocery bag in each arm.

A bit startled, I turned quickly to look at her and tried to smile. "I don't know, Grammie...I really don't know about that," I said.

Aunt Doris drove me to Knoxville for my first follow-up appointment, and on the way back to Grantville, we talked. She told me that Miss Bertie called her regularly to ask about me and that whenever I was ready, I could start going up the hill to the big house so that Miss Bertie could help me do some refresher work at the piano. It was all up to me, Aunt Doris said.

Between you and me, I was stunned. After everything that had happened, after I had pretty much shown myself to be a full-blown, ungrateful, drunken- psycho, semi-criminal little fool, these women—Momma, Grammie, Aunt Doris, and Miss Bertie—still believed in me. I rode the rest of the way home in silence, humbled, yet again, and amazed.

⤙◯

On a hot Sunday afternoon in July, E. A. drove me back to Chattanooga from Hammondsville. I had come from Grantville by bus on Thursday for her bridal tea that Saturday, which, from what I could tell, had been the social event of the summer in that little corner of northwest Georgia. It was a good thing, given how much stuff E. A. received at that tea, that she and Everett could afford a big house.

"Now, Grace...I really want you to come back at least a week before the wedding, OK?" She was driving her dad's Buick much more carefully than she had ever driven her Corvette.

"OK, E. A., I will...now will my dress be sent to your house or to Grantville?"

I, and the six other attendants, had been measured by the bridal-store owner who had come to Hammondsville from Atlanta.

"It will be sent to you...I suppose your aunt could do any alterations?" E. A. asked.

I had to laugh.

"Are you kidding, E. A? My aunt Doris could have *made* the dress." I chuckled.

We were getting closer to the bus station; E. A. suddenly sighed and took a deep breath. I knew something was coming.

"Grace...I've been in touch with Janelle several times this summer," she said.

At the mention of anybody or anything about Vanderbilt, my heart sank a little lower again. The thought of my last months there, of what I had thrown away, of how I had behaved—all of it made me sick every time it came- up. I worked at pushing those thoughts --and memories-- to the depths of my mind.

But now I couldn't get away...I was in a moving car with someone who knew the details, the very worst of it all, and I couldn't stop her from talking. Whatever she was going to say, I had to hear it.

"She's glad you're doing better...she says you're one of her all-time very favorites, you know?" E. A. said as I looked out the window, away from her, and didn't say a word.

"So....Janelle wanted me to tell you that your scholarship is being held open. She says that means that the Music Department has not returned it to the dean's pool. Dr. Heller told Janelle that he wants to see if you'll come back...come back and finish. Apparently he can allow that when there's been..." She groped for words here. "...when there's been an emergency...or something."

I kept staring out the window as E. A. pulled into the parking lot at the Greyhound station and parked. We sat there for a while in silence.

"Grace?"

I didn't answer.

"Grace?" she said again.

I knew her well enough to know that she'd say it fifty-five more times straight if I didn't respond, so I turned and looked at her.

"Grace, you know you could do it...you could go back and start fresh and probably do much better... given that you wouldn't have *my* dumbass distractin' you."

I had to laugh out loud at that comment: E. A. as my dumbass distraction? There was maybe a little bit of truth in that.

"So, Grace...why not think about it? OK? Just think...if you go back and get your degree, then you could move to Atlanta...there's bound to be all kinds of music jobs there."

I looked E. A. straight in the face; her eyes shined with hope--- true, undeterred hope. To her, nothing was out of reach, nothing was out of the question. She meant every word she was saying, and she really cared. This girl-- this young woman-- who had stuck by me while I firebombed my life, sincerely cared about me.

I nodded my head ever so slightly, but it was enough for her.

"You'll think about it?" she asked, wide-eyed and eager.

I nodded again.

"Ohhhhh, Grace...I'm so happy." She reached to hug me. "I know you can do it! I can't wait to tell Janelle."

Before I walked up the steps to the bus, E. A. hugged me again.

"I can't stand it, Grace! Just think...only three and a half more weeks! I can't wait for you to see my dress!"

From my window seat on the bus, I waved to E. A., and she blew me kisses. As friends went, I knew I'd never have another one like her—but I never saw her again.

The following week, I spent two whole days helping Grammie. We put-up fourteen quarts of tomatoes and eight quarts of green beans and still had peas and peaches to do. I sat with her late one evening on the back porch, shelling peas; in the distance we could see the glow of the baseball-park lights, where Wesley was playing in a summer tournament.

Sometimes, just out of the blue, Grammie would sigh deeply and look toward the ball fields. Before Sometimes, just out of the blue, Grammie would sigh deeply and look toward the ball fields. Before that summer, I probably wouldn't have even noticed such a little thing, but now I did. Experience, and some hard-earned sensitivity, had matured me. Now I didn't take so much for granted...especially the people who loved me

"Whatcha thinkin' about, Grammie?" I asked, reaching in the basket for another handful of purple hulls.

She glanced over at me but then looked away.

"Ohhh...I was just thinkin' about your daddy...how much I miss him and how I bet he'd just love to see Wesley playin' ball," she said.

"Yeah...he *would* like that, wouldn't he?"

I nodded and kept shelling. After a few moments, I spoke.

"Grammie, where do you think he is?" I don't think I had ever asked that question of her or Aunt Doris, and I *knew* I had never asked Momma.

There was another pause.

"Honey, I don't know, but I'll tell you a secret." She reached for more peas. "Hoyt's my boy, and I love him...and I hope-- wherever he is-- he's safe and happy...but I decided a long time ago that maybe it's been for the best that he wasn't here."

That comment, coming from my grandmother, was a stunner.

"Why, Grammie? Why do you say that?"

Grammie set her big, old wooden shellin' bowl down and wiped her hands on her apron. Then she reached over and took the metal bowl off my lap and put it down, too.

"Grace, go inside and get us two big glasses of iced tea...there's lemon in the icebox. Then come back, and sit with me. It's time I told you a few things."

That was the night I heard it all—all about Grandpa Billy's drinking and fighting and hell-raising and all about my daddy's sad young life. Grammie told me that the day Wesley was born, her heart sank, because she was so afraid her Hoyt would do to his son what Grandpa

Billy had done to him. She said the daughters were different for the Stevens men...it was the *sons* who caught all the hell. I knew Grammie mainly meant the punching and strapping, but I knew firsthand that the hell part also included the screaming and cussing, the *words* that had so deeply scarred all of us.

"So, Grace, when your daddy took-off like he did, I was heartbroken, but I told myself then that at least things might be better for Wesley... that with Hoyt out of the picture, Wes might be better off in the long run."

Tears filled Grammie's eyes, and she looked away, into the night sky.

"And all this time I was worried about Wesley... never dreamin' it'd be you. You were always so good, Gracie...I just never dreamed the liquor would get *you*." Grammie wiped tears from her cheeks with the edge of her apron.

I lay awake for most of that night, thinking back on so much, piecing together the missing links and loose ends that Grammie—that *somebody, thank God*—had at last provided.

All of a sudden, I understood; I understood why Aunt Doris was the way she was, preferring to live her life without a man at all rather than risk getting one like her daddy or her brother, and why she and Grammie hated alcohol in any form or fashion. I saw the root of my daddy's drinking and selfish irresponsibility and how that one line from him that echoed in my head had to have come to him from someone else: *who do you think you are anyway?*

Didn't that line just sum it all up? In other words, just don't get to thinking that you're worth much or that you're anything special or that life's gonna be any better for you. And hadn't I eventually stumbled upon the cure for that painful echo—liquor? The very same solution I guess my daddy had found.

Around daybreak Momma's alarm went off, and she crept into the bathroom to get ready to go open the Buddy Burger. I lay still in the dark and just watched her move, dressing quietly to not wake me up.

Momma-- she had never once asked me anything about what had happened, never once scolded me or gotten angry. She and I had just picked- up right where we'd left off before I'd ever gone to Vandy. I really wondered what she thought of me, because now I knew-- more clearly than ever-- what I thought of her.

Grammie probably had to look at things her own way in order to live with it all, and that was fine. But I knew now another reason my daddy had taken off—it was Momma.

Momma was no Grammie. Momma was *not* going to stand for what Grammie had put-up with. Momma gave Hoyt Stevens tit for tat and then some; Momma *did* believe that a person's life could get better. My momma was tougher, in the long run, than Billy or Hoyt Stevens ever thought about being.

As I heard Momma's little Corvair pull out of the driveway, I thought about what would have happened if my daddy had ever decided he'd take a belt or a strap to Wesley. Good God Almighty, I knew without a doubt what would have happened: without any hesitation, Momma would have put herself between Wesley and Daddy—and I think she might have even done the same for me. Momma would have killed to protect us. Words and arguments were one thing, but for her, fists and straps would have been altogether another.

No, Momma was not Grammie; she was not going to kowtow for any man, and Daddy knew it. For Hoyt Stevens, Arlene Connors had been hellfire on two legs, smokin' a Lucky, and *that* was what he couldn't live with. My grandmother, a soft, sweet woman, had been no match for the Stevens men, but Momma? She was a different story, and because of her both Wesley and I had a chance—a chance at a different, better life.

The next day I sat down at my piano again. I went back to basics: Hanon. I played hour after hour of Hanon. It was exhausting, because I had to concentrate completely on every single note, every finger, and every detail that I had once known without having to think about. *Then* it had been easy—*now* it was hard work.

But I had made up my mind—before I walked up the hill and started music lessons again with Miss Bertie, I was going to get myself back on track. By God, I didn't come from women who quit, and if Vanderbilt would have me, I was going back.

15

~

Everett Belcher was a good pilot, they said, but he did not have the experience to fly through the freak thunderstorm that blew in and turned—against all predictions—southeast instead of northeast on that Monday morning in August. His small single-engine plane, carrying him, E. A., and the last of her belongings from the apartment went down in the mountains of north Georgia, just eight hundred yards short of an open field.

There was no fire, but according to the people who finally reached the scene nearly two hours later, there was nothing left of that airplane. Turbulence, poor visibility, lightning, pilot error, mechanical failure—all of it was mentioned, but it didn't really matter. The golden couple, the perfect, young lovers who had the world on a string, died together in the remote treetops of Catoosa County, Georgia.

Instead of packing my suitcase to go to my best friend's wedding, I packed it to go to her funeral.

That Monday afternoon I had walked to the drugstore to pick-up some things. I was walking down Oakdale, about three blocks from home, when I saw Wesley on his bicycle, riding toward me. He had his baseball cleats and his glove draped over the handlebars. He circled me several times as he spoke.

"Grammie sent me to find you...she wants you to come straight home," he said.

"I *am* going straight home...what's wrong?" I was concerned. "Is she OK?"

He made one last circle and said, "Yeah, I guess so...she was callin' Aunt Doris when I left...I gotta get to practice," he said and sped away.

At the next corner I turned left, so I could cut through Mrs. Barnes's yard and get to Grammie's faster.

All I can tell you is that I sat for several hours at the kitchen table. I heard Grammie tell it all two more times—once to Aunt Doris and again to Momma—how a neighbor-lady of the Hammondses was with the family and they had her making phone calls for them. There were no details yet about the service, but someone would be calling back.

Grammie was the only one who was crying—although she had never met Ellis Ann Hammonds, the mere idea that my good friend, a beautiful, young woman set to be wed, had died so tragically was enough. I just sat there, and I honestly can't tell you any more than that. Evidently it just wouldn't sink in; I couldn't believe what I was hearing.

By nine o'clock that night, I was standing on a stool while Aunt Doris pinned up a hem on me; from her fabric stash she had snatched a piece of midnight-blue linen and was at work on a plain three-quarter-sleeve dress for me to wear. Momma said she'd pick up some dark stockings for me the next day. Grammie washed and ironed some of my other things, while Momma checked on the bus schedule to get me back to Hammondsville. The three of them seemed to switch to automatic, just quietly doing whatever had to be done, while I just stood around in a pale trance.

The trance ended the next day when, around noon, the mailman delivered a large box and, without even thinking, I opened it; inside was my burnt-gold satin maid-of-honor dress. I dropped to my knees right there in Grammie's living room, sobbing.

All of a sudden the images that had been floating around in my head came into sharp, horrible focus, and I saw it: I saw that little plane, I saw E. A. and Everett together, and then I saw her clothes and shoes and books strewn through the treetops as that plane disintegrated. And then I knew it—my best friend was gone. E. A. was gone.

Wayne Tayloe and his cousin Skip were going to the funeral; Wayne called and said he would pick me up in Knoxville, if I didn't mind riding with him and Skip in the truck. Aunt Doris drove me to Knoxville to meet him at seven Thursday morning. We arrived at Harmony Methodist Church in Hammondsville at one o'clock that afternoon.

Not having attended that many funerals, I wasn't a good judge of things, but Wayne immediately said there were at least a thousand people there. The church was full, and there were people standing outside the open doors at the front and the side. There was special seating for the people who would have been in the wedding. The other attendants were Chi Os from Vandy and three of E. A.'s cousins. And the flowers... my God, the flowers were everywhere—but the only thing on the closed white casket was a garland of heather and orange blossoms, attached to E. A.'s wedding veil that lay on top.

One of the most pitiful things I've ever seen was E. A.'s daddy, Mr. Hammonds. He sat between LaLa and Mrs. Hammonds, and between the two of them, they barely managed to keep the man upright through the service. He was beside himself, out of his head with grief. Tommy insisted on being a pallbearer; he stared at the floor as tears streamed down his face. It was all a nightmare. I kept thinking, hoping, that we were in a play or some kind of crazy movie and that in a second it would be over.

At the cemetery a group of us—some of her friends from Vandy—stood back and waited while they closed E. A.'s grave. The family had gone, and only a few people were still there as the sun dropped in the hot summer sky.

Wayne glanced at his watch.

"Grace, we probably need to leave if you're gonna get that nine-fifteen bus out of Chattanooga," he said.

I nodded and vaguely motioned toward the grave; he understood. I just wanted a minute to walk back over there.

With the sea of flowers, it was difficult to actually tell exactly where the dirt pile was, but it appeared to be the fourth spot from the edge of the big marble marker that simply said "HAMMONDS." E. A. was beside her grandparents and a maiden aunt who had died young. Eventually she'd have an individual footstone like the others.

I bent down, and from one of the huge wreaths, I pulled an apricot-tinted rose. Her wedding colors were burnt- gold, apricot, and ivory.

"Oh, Grace...ohhhhh, Grace..." How many times had I heard her say that? Whether we were laughing or fussing or whatever, she always said it the same way, "Ohhhhh, Grace." I wanted so much for it all to be wrong, for it to be some huge mistake, and for her to walk up behind me and say, "Ohhhhh, Grace," and then I'd turn, and she'd smile at me.

A minute or so later, I took my rose, and swallowing my tears, I walked away.

On the way to Chattanooga, Skip fell asleep, and Wayne and I talked.

Wayne had seen Everett only once or twice, there around the apartment in Nashville.

"He seemed like a nice guy...too bad he wasn't a better pilot," he said.

From the way he said that, I could tell that Wayne was not surprised or shocked or wiped- out at the idea of two young people-- with their whole lives ahead of them-- being just up and gone. Wayne wasn't matter-of-fact about it—it just *was what it was* to him.

"Hell's bells, Grace...good people get snatched off this planet every day—right and left—and plenty of them never got to do half of what Ellis and Everett did...so keep that in mind, and don't take anything for granted, my friend. None of us know how much time we have—only a fool lets any of it go to waste."

Wayne was right. He was so right it made me want to cry. Wayne's life experiences had already propelled him years ahead of most twenty-five-year-olds. He had already seen more than his share of death and loss and waste that couldn't be undone or rewound. What must he think of me, I suddenly wondered, feeling small and silly.

At the bus station, he walked me inside and looked all around.

"I think you'll be OK in here for twenty minutes," he decided, placing my bag on the bench.

"Thanks, Wayne...I'll be fine."

He hugged me and then said, almost in a whisper, "I'm really sorry about what happened to Ellis...I know she loved you a lot."

I nodded and bit my lip; I couldn't speak for fear that I'd start bawling.

He stepped away and hitched up his pants, a constant habit of his.

"OK then...stay in touch, Gracie," Wayne said. "And look me up if you get back to Nashville anytime soon."

I waved and tried to smile. "I will Wayne."

In mid- September I walked up the hill to Miss Bertie's. She was waiting for me at the open front door and threw out her arms. I immediately noticed that she had lost more weight—her clothes sort of hung on her now.

"Grace, my darling girl...it is so wonderful to see you." She stood with her hands on my shoulders. "You look just fabulous...you really do," she said.

As we walked out of the foyer, she put her arm around me and then suddenly stopped. "And, Grace, I want to tell you now how very sorry I was to hear about your friend Ellis. She was a lovely, lovely girl, and it's just beyond comprehension...just heartbreaking...that something like that could happen," Miss Bertie said sincerely.

I just nodded my head, because I really didn't know what to say.

We had soup, cucumber sandwiches, and iced tea in the sun-room, and then we went into the studio, where nothing had changed. For a second I was eleven years old again—nervous and unsure of myself.

So that's how it all began again, but this time there were no envelopes of money or references to my family background. It was work... work to get back what I had thrown away, work to find myself again and to regain some footing in what had so graciously come to me and had once mattered so much.

At the end of that first day, Miss Bertie was clearly tired; when she walked me to the door, she reached out and rested her hand on my shoulder.

"Grace...I want you to promise me something."

I turned and looked at her.

"I want you to promise me that you'll never walk away from the piano again—never, not for anything or anybody. The piano is who you are. Your gift must *never* be wasted... so please, don't ever let it go again."

I knew she was right. I took a deep breath and paused, reminding myself of everyone I had let down. It was not hard to make that promise.

"I promise, Miss Bertie."

Three mornings a week, for two hours, from September through mid-December, I was at Miss Bertie's. At noontime when I left, she rested before her afternoon students arrived, and I went to the Kress store and worked. Then at night I was at my piano at Grammie's again for two hours.

It did not take long for my mind to get right again, for my balance and my sanity to start a remarkable comeback. Maybe you think it was just the medications I was on, but I think it was the piano. More slowly, my technique and memory re-emerged, and with them came purpose and my sense of worth.

One night, just before Christmas, I played "Turkish March" with as much skill and finesse as I had ever played it. It damn near brought me to tears.

After many phone calls and letters and a trip to Vanderbilt to sit down with Dr. Heller, my scholarship was reinstated. On a freezing-cold, clear day in early January, Momma and R. T. drove me to campus in R. T.'s big Oldsmobile.

I was lucky enough to get assigned to a senior dorm, although I was still technically a junior; it was one of the oldest buildings on campus that had been renovated. I took one of five private rooms on the fourth floor, which had once been the attic. Those rooms were the last to go, because they stayed so hot most of the time. R. T. said, if necessary, he'd send one of his sons over in the spring with a little window air- conditioner. But that day in January, my little attic dorm room was perfect.

There were numerous places in Nashville I never set foot in again: all the Vanderbilt fraternity and sorority houses, the dorm and the apartment building where E. A. and I had lived, the Hermitage Hotel, and Cumberland Country Club. I knew better than to even go near them. You couldn't have gotten me in any of those places at gunpoint, and on the rare occasion that a sharp memory or a flashback popped into my head, I sometimes ended-up feeling like it had all happened to somebody else, some other Grace Stevens.

To say I buckled down is probably an understatement; I was on a mission not only to make-up for some things but to excel at *everything*.

Most of my original year group was gone, which was not a bad thing, because I was in a whole new class of mostly new faces and new talent. By the end of that winter semester, I had several good friends at the dorm and in the Music Department. Janelle and Dr. Heller kept me busy the following summer with part-time work, while I went to summer school.

With all that, and preparing for my senior performance—every music-education major was required to present a solo recital of pieces preapproved by the department —the time flew by. Before I knew it, fall semester started, and if everything went well, I'd graduate from Vanderbilt University in May, only one year late.

16
~

Early one morning, in March of my senior year, my phone rang; it was Aunt Doris. I knew it had to be bad news for her to be calling at that hour, and I was right.

Miss Bertie had put up quite a battle, but the cancer that had started in her breast was fatal; they had done everything they knew to do, but it just kept coming back, first one place and then another. When I'd seen her at Christmas, she'd only weighed about one hundred pounds but was still in good spirits.

Cooper told me then that sometimes when she was really weak, he would just scoop her up in his big arms, like a little kitten, he said, and take her upstairs or move her around the house. He said one afternoon he was carrying her up the stairs, and when she said something about Rhett carrying Scarlett upstairs, they both started laughing so hard he nearly dropped her. Momma said she'd have given her best frying pan to have seen that.

Miss Bertie and Aunt Doris and Laura Holderness had, together, become a triple threat in Grantville, which some people loved and others absolutely despised. They sponsored some women's groups about political issues and voting, and they started a much-needed Mothers' Morning Out program at the Episcopal church, which accepted *all* children—black, white, rich, poor—all of 'em.

And, by the way, did I tell you what Miss Bertie had done a while back?

Frances Walker

Included in her piano students now were two little colored girls—
no, two little *black* girls. One of them was Lydadelle's niece, and the
other one was a little girl from way out in the county who had been
badly burned as a baby and was horribly scarred. The child loved music,
and Cooper was sent every week to bring her to Miss Bertie's. That
really honked off some of the parents, but Miss Bertie told them that
they were all welcome to terminate their children's music lessons if
they wished. Only one did. Momma kept wishin' that Miss Bertie would
just do what she would have done-- told 'em all to, "Kiss my ass."

So now Aunt Doris was telling me that the end was near and that I
needed to get home if I could. She said Miss Bertie really wanted to see
me. I caught the Greyhound at noon.

You may have wondered by now—or maybe you hadn't even
thought about it—why there's been no mention at all of that Brahms's
Intermezzo Op.118 that Miss Bertie played back in 1925? Yeah, I'd wondered about that piece of music, too.

Beneath the photograph of her in the white dress was a framed
copy of the program from that night; that was the only way I even knew
what she had performed. Miss Bertie had never suggested the Brahms
to me; we had never listened to it on her stereo, and she had certainly
never played it for me. I got the feeling that, for some reason, it was a
no-no, so I just ignored it.

I ignored it until that January when I returned to Vandy. In my first
meeting with my new Music Department advisor, Mr. Cobb told me it
was time to start giving some thought to the music for my senior performance. Mr. Cobb, we all called him Cobbie, reached behind him to
the messy, overloaded shelves of music books, stacks of sheet music,
and piles of music magazines and somehow quickly produced a copy
of the Brahms's Intermezzos, A Minor and A Major. As I glanced over
it, he assured me that if I started right now I *might*, given all my other
courses, have it ready to present in fourteen months.

So I took it on, and I never said a word to anybody. Knowing that
Miss Bertie would be attending my senior performance along with my
family, I planned to make the Brahms my final piece and to dedicate it

182

in the program to Roberta Dabney Hewitt. My goal was to simply do it a respectful justice, for her, because I figured it must have some special meaning to her and I wanted to surprise her. Perhaps to her that particular piece symbolized the pinnacle of her own beauty and talent in that other world so long ago. I didn't really know for sure.

And as it turned out, I'd never know.

Momma met me at eight thirty that night at the Grantville bus depot.

"She's gone, Grace...died around four o'clock this afternoon," Momma said quietly, taking my suitcase from me.

I didn't say a word, and I didn't cry as we walked to the car.

Around the kitchen at Miss Bertie's that night, some sitting and others standing, we gathered. There was Grammie and Aunt Doris, Laura Holderness, R. T., Evelyn, Cooper, Lydadelle, and, of all people, Hughie Renfroe. I had to look twice to recognize Hughie—he had gained at least sixty pounds. Momma commented later that Hughie had decided to eat his way to completing that accounting degree his daddy wanted him to have.

They told me how Miss Bertie had gotten worse yesterday afternoon but refused to go back to the hospital, saying that she couldn't take anymore needles or machines. Evelyn sat with her through the night, and Aunt Doris relieved her this morning after she'd called me.

Miss Bertie wouldn't even take any sips of the ginger ale she had come to like and was very still and quiet until around noon, when she suddenly sat up and called for Cooper. She wanted him to bring her a Meissen figurine, something that had belonged to her grandmother and that had sat forever on the mantle above the living-room fireplace.

"It's very old...and not really very pretty, but I want to give it to Grace when she gets here," Miss Bertie said.

So now, on the kitchen table, sat a small creamy porcelain figure of a barefoot young woman in a long dress, holding some sort of big jug or bottle on her shoulder; the whole thing was maybe ten inches tall. We were all looking at it, a little baffled.

Mrs. Holderness spoke.

"That's a nineteenth-century German piece...I think it's *Rebecca at the Well.*" She looked up at me. "I wonder why she wanted you to have that, Grace?"

I stared at the thing and shook my head. I didn't think I had ever even noticed it

"I have no idea, Mrs. Holderness."

Miss Bertie's niece in Richmond had been called and would arrive the next afternoon. Mrs. Holderness was the only one who had ever met this niece, so she volunteered to be at the house when she arrived.

"But first thing in the morning, I'm calling the Blossom Shop myself...I want that front door draped in crepe and lilies. I don't care what the niece says."

It was done by noon the next day.

Hughie agreed to contact the newspaper, and Aunt Doris said that she and Grammie would help Evelyn with all the food that would start pouring in tomorrow. By midnight, we all figured it was time to close up the house and leave.

Cooper and R. T. went upstairs to turn off everything. Evelyn and Hughie both started sobbing and hanging on each other, which caused Momma to just walk outside and wait at the car; Lydadelle followed her out.

"Grace, would you go check the front door?" Mrs. Holderness asked as she pulled on her coat.

For some reason, I reached over and picked up the *Rebecca* statue as I said, "Yes, ma'am."

Carrying the figurine casually with me, I walked through the dining room toward the foyer, past the big Feurich piano. I locked the front door and then turned out the foyer lights. Standing beneath the entrance arch to the living room, I paused and smiled at the memory of my eighteenth birthday party. I hated to think of the house left in total darkness, so I decided to leave on the crystal lamp in the living room.

I stood there, looking around at all Miss Bertie's lovely things; it was so sad. I knew that at one time her things had meant a lot to her, but she had changed. I wondered where all that finery would end- up, what the niece would do with all of it.

As I started back toward the kitchen, I noticed that one of the lamps in the studio was on, so I went to turn it off. Then I remembered--- that lamp switch was broken so I'd have to stretch down to unplug the lamp at the outlet, so I placed *Rebecca* on the piano bench, on the side nearest me. Glancing down directly into the jug she was holding, I suddenly noticed there was something in there. I picked up the figurine, and finally, after shaking and digging, I got it out. *What in the world*, I wondered.

Rolled into a tight, wrinkled scroll was a small envelope, and I could see that there was something written on it. Finally I tugged and unrolled it enough to see. In black ink was written,

"For G's 1st music lesson."

It was Aunt Doris's handwriting, and inside was a ten-dollar bill and two singles.

I flashed back to that Thursday afternoon so long ago. I remembered exactly what I had on; I remembered the smell of burning leaves in the air and how nervous I'd been, and I remembered Mrs. Hewitt rushing out of the room after I handed her that envelope.

Looking out the window now, I could see Momma standing out by the car. I wondered what she'd say if she knew what Mrs. Hewitt had said to me that day, and I wondered what Miss Bertie really thought of all that had happened since then.

Glancing up, I caught a fuzzy reflection of myself in the window-pane; my strand of pearls from Miss Bertie lay perfectly against my navy-blue cardigan. Yes, there was so much, so very much to remember. I sat down on the piano bench, and, clutching the figurine, I leaned against the keyboard and sobbed. I was certain Momma saw me through the window, but that was OK. It was all finally OK.

17

~

Well, how much more babblin' are you willin' to listen to? Because I could go on and on, but let's be honest—at this point I should just hit the high spots for you.

First, you wouldn't believe—not in your wildest dreams—how much Grantville changed. The steel mill held on until the late 1980s, when cheap, foreign steel basically killed so many companies. The good news is that Aunt Doris got herself a pretty good pension after her thirty-four years at Crocker-Hewitt.

Then, not two years after the mill closed, who came to town but a bunch of Japanese businessmen, bowing and grinning in every direction. Before anybody could turn around, there was a compact-car factory being built and a parts plant for electronics that were made in Grantville, shipped to Japan for assembly, and then shipped back to the United States. Momma said every time she turned on her television, she figured the "dang thang" had seen more of the world than she'd ever see.

And speaking of Momma, it took nearly three years, but Momma got a divorce and married R. T. Stancil, which by then didn't surprise anybody, but what happened next sure *did* surprise *everybody*. Momma quit smokin'. Can you believe it? Gave 'em up, cold turkey, after all those years. She gained fifteen pounds, but R. T. said he'd rather have her pudgy than puffin', so that was that.

Oh...and she went back and got her GED. Wesley and Momma graduated from high school the same year, and, yes, it made the *Grantville*

Journal. For her graduation gift, R. T. bought Momma a whole set of blue-and-white dishes, made in England.

R. T. sold the Buddy Burger to Wendy's. They tore down the old building, which certainly needed tearing down, and with the money, R. T. and Momma remodeled their house in Crestview and bought a huge motor home. Now they cruise around, going in whatever direction they feel like, "burnin' gasoline like it's city water," Momma says. She says her job at the Buddy Burger changed her life. I guess she forgets sometimes that it changed mine and Wesley's, too.

Wesley? Well, to Momma's great relief, Wesley made peace with R. T., partly because his twins were happy to see their dad married and were so good, right from the start, to Momma and Wesley. The twins took Wesley to several football games at UT, took him duck hunting up in Virginia, and later on helped him fix-up an old Ford he bought. I can't really say that Wesley ever got over Daddy leaving, but as it turned out, he ended up with three big brothers, if you count R. T.

And baseball did get Wesley into college, but he just couldn't stick with it. He got through one year at Carson-Newman before he quit and went back home. A few years later, R. T. paid for him to go down to Atlanta to a special school; he became an aircraft mechanic, and he's done really well. Wes married the youngest Holloway girl, and they've got three wonderful boys-—three wild Indians, according to Aunt Doris, but she says that about all boys.

Wes is a really good daddy, and wouldn't you know it—just like Momma—he'll drink a cold beer once in a while and then just leave it at that. Anything more never crosses his mind.

So...almost all the big houses up in Riverview are gone now. There are some fancy, gated condo neighborhoods up there, one of which stands where the Hewitt house once was. Some brave soul bought Judge Roberts's old place and turned it into a bed and breakfast, and believe it or not, folks from up north actually come by and stay there, paying six dollars for a bowl of cheese grits. Have you ever?

Aunt Doris took the money Bertie El left her and bought a house in Crestview for her and Grammie. It's a cute, little place, all on one level, with two bathrooms, which never ceases to thrill Aunt Doris. Apparently having her own bathroom had been her heart's secret desire for years.

Grammie got to have a dishwasher, a microwave oven, and a clothes dryer—and she enjoyed every minute of them until she died at age eighty-eight. My grandmother always kept the same picture of my daddy on her bedside table; in it he is maybe nineteen years old, wearing a plaid shirt and a baseball cap, and although he is smiling, there is a hard, distant look in his eyes.

When she died, Grammie never knew that Daddy had died six months earlier, drunk, on the back of a motorcycle that the Houston police estimated left the road doing over 90 m.p.h.

"No...I'm not about to tell her," Aunt Doris said. "'Cause how could she ever make any sense out of her fifty-nine-year-old son dyin' like *that*?"

I couldn't have agreed more. It was good that Grammie died still hoping that her boy was happy and safe somewhere.

Miss Bertie left a trust fund that put Lydadelle's niece through college, and she set up annuities for Evelyn and Cooper, and she paid for the little burned girl to have four different operations over ten years with a specialist in Atlanta.

And I know what you're thinking now—what about me?

Well, as if Miss Bertie hadn't already done enough for me, she had one last ace up her lace sleeve. For years, every single dollar that was paid to Bertie El Hewitt for my music lessons was put aside, into an investment account in the name of Grace Stevens. That fat, little nest egg, along with some of Miss Bertie's treasures, came to me, and, yes, I do think of them as treasures.

I graduated with honors from Vandy and got a job as a music teacher in a nice private school in Knoxville. I worked there for ten years, and I gave music lessons on the side to as many children as I could fit-in every afternoon. That was how I met the man I married.

One of my students said her uncle Allen was a lawyer, but he really wanted to learn to play the piano; would I teach him? Allen Forsythe and

I were married a year later but not before I sat him down and told him *everything*—every nasty detail from start to finish. He never wavered.

Wayne Tayloe, married and teaching high school English in Conecuh County, Alabama, came to my wedding and finally claimed his dance with me. He and Allen have become good friends.

My son, Allen Jr., is fourteen years old, and my daughter, Dabney Ellis, called Dee since she was three days old, is ten now. She loves soccer and Chopin. When Dee was born, it took me three days to name her—there were so many names I wanted to use.

By then I only dreamed about E. A. occasionally, unlike those first years after she died, when I dreamed about her at least once or twice a month. My second night in the hospital OB wing, I slept soundly and walked with E. A.—seems like it was on a trail or somewhere on the Vandy campus—and I told her I wanted to name my baby girl after her. She laughed and nodded, and as clear as could be, I heard her say, "Ohhhhh, Grace."

In the corner of our basement is a stack of boxes. At first Allen wanted to know what was in them that was so valuable that I had dragged them around with me everywhere; I told him they were just stuff—stuff I wanted to keep in case we ever had a daughter, and happily, now we do.

The boxes remain, and sometimes Dee asks again what's in them and when are we going to open them? I tell her again that we will someday...when she's older. I want to wait until I can tell her about some things. I just don't want to risk her not understanding or maybe brushing it all off as so much old junk.

I couldn't stand that, because the contents of those boxes are a big part of Dee's legacy: Grammie's recipe box, aprons, and scrapbooks; a box of Aunt Doris's patterns and some of her embroidery; the Biddle silver teaspoons; my first black dress; Miss Bertie's Limoges china and her silver tea set; and, of course, Momma's stuff—her Buddy Burger uniform, a picture of her with Edna and Lydadelle behind the counter, a picture of her alone standing beside her little blue Corvair. And lastly there's my maid-of-honor dress for E. A.'s wedding—still with the tags on it, wrapped in tissue paper. Beneath the dress is an old Chi Omega T-shirt that she loved, and with it is the dried apricot-tinted rose from her grave, pressed in wax paper.

Everything in those boxes—every last piece of it—has meaning and value, whether anybody else thinks so or not.

In a large, spacious room above our three-car garage, I have a studio where I teach piano. In it I have the two pianos from Mrs. Hewitt's studio, and I have the Baldwin that came to me from Mrs. Holderness. I have shelves and cabinets full of music, all kinds. It is, no doubt, worse than Cobbie's office at Vandy.

Above my desk are probably two dozen certificates, photos, and plaques, but the one right in the center is the anchor for all the others: it is the picture of a "Miss Dabney of Richmond, Virginia, on stage at the National Theatre" in 1925. Most of my students never even notice it. To them it is just a relic, an old black-and-white photograph, from an ancient time, of a thin, young girl in a plain white dress, standing beside a piano. But not a day goes by that I don't glance at that picture and feel lucky...so lucky, all over again.

Sometimes in the evening, when I'm home alone, I walk into the living room and switch on the lamp between the two armchairs. There's no room for a sofa or other furniture in there. I sit down at Miss Bertie's fine, glossy Feurich, which takes up most of our suburban living room, and I play. I play Chopin and Mozart and even "Beulah Land."

But I always finish with the Brahms Intermezzo in A Major.

I play it for Miss Bertie, while *Rebecca at the Well* stands safely nearby on a shelf, holding her jug—still with its meager contents tucked inside. Beside the figurine is the silver-framed photo of me and E. A. on that November Saturday so long ago.

So that's it. In the end, it's the small things, isn't it? It's the little reminders of the ones who mattered most, the ones who made a difference—the women who might have looked fragile but were strong and tough and never quit believing.

For me, and for Dee, that is the greatest legacy.

END

31856688R00120

Made in the USA
Lexington, KY
28 April 2014